Thin

A Novel

by

Sadhana Seelam

Just because something doesn't do what you planned it to do, doesn't mean it's useless.

- Thomas Edison

ACKNOWLEDGMENTS

I thank my parents Y.S. Anand Reddy and
Y.S. Susheela Reddy who taught me that to be
good at anything, you have to first, be good.

CHAPTER ONE

An unseasonably warm New York sun burned the shiny center of Stephen Baylor's smooth bare head as he juggled a bulging computer bag, held his phone against his ear with his shoulder and a clutch of newspapers under his other arm. Mostly engrossed in a lawyerly conversation with the same colleague who had called him for the third time that morning, and it wasn't even 11:00 am yet for Pete's sake!

Stephen was soon riveted by an excellent pair of legs making their way on the crowded sidewalk putting one enticing leg in front of another with calculated allure. His eyes climbed the length of her body noting that this svelte creature was a very tall brunette. He didn't know if it was the extra high heels in shocking pink she was wearing under a gray dress that swished tantalizingly above her knees that had so transfixed his attention or the sheer beauty of a great pair of legs. Distractions of this size and form never came in small measures Stephen admitted to himself regretfully. *"Man oh man"* he muttered, marveling that only in New York could you see legs like that, the shapeliness, how slim they were and those *'fuck me now'* shoes... No kidding. Only in New York.

Just when he was weighed down by not just his various bags and files but by this fellow on the other end who wouldn't hang up, this impossibly real person stopped at a vendor selling earrings to look curiously at some of the wares he was hawking. So absorbed was he by this vision in front of him, Stephen barely managed to skip a large puddle of water that had collected in the uneven patches of pavement following the fantastic freak storm from the night before and he dropped his phone. Cursing he bent down to pick up his cascading possessions, chastened by the ungainly patch of water. By the time he looked up, the apparition had disappeared leaving him with a memory of the gray chiffon dress swishing at the knees, high above the pink pumps. He sighed, stopped in front of the glass façade of the building to straighten his tie and walked into the mega multi-rise where his office was located.

His raised eyebrows bore testimony to the fierce argument he was having with himself. Of course he excused New York, it was a beautiful city, no matter that there were uneven pavement spots that acted as a spoiler to what could have been a potentially romantic interlude on what portended to be a mediocre day at best.

Geographically, Stephen's circle of experience didn't include too many places. Having gone to Yale for an undergraduate degree and on to Columbia to get his law degree, his decades since college had been dedicated to developing his career. He had begun by launching into a rigorous internship and getting sucked into the ridiculously long hours at work and consequently had never had the time to go to places other than to Denver because it was home base and more recently to San Francisco fairly frequently, following the acquisition of a large client in the exciting South of Market area.

San Francisco had happened on a whim initially when he offered to sit in for a colleague, and then after cultivating a client base there, he became a regular and soon an old timer, knowing all the restaurants, managing to sit next to the coveted window most nights at dinner. Among the first things Stephen noticed in San Francisco was that perhaps due to all those hills, it was no surprise the women were *almost* as slim, or *slimmer than* women in New York? Dare he *think* it, New York?? The thought was blasphemous, if not to anyone else, to him. It was a question of infidelity and here he was clearly transgressing, he felt a flush of consternation wash over him.

Stephen pushed San Francisco out of his mind with an almost physical force. He wasn't looking forward to the meeting with Judy, Ryan and this new Indian attorney Anil who had joined them from a competing firm. Stephen's initial reaction to Anil was to dismiss him as a know-it-all. Lately however he had started to like his spontaneity and unabashed humor. Sure enough Anil was headed down when Stephen got off the elevator, "Hey Stephen, see you in a bit." Anil said in an unmistakable American accent with something of a Philadelphia/Northeast twang. Stephen wondered at that. How was it possible that Anil, with that excessive facial hair, Anil sported a short moustache, and those black, black eyes, fringed by a brush of lashes, blinking every time a thick lock of hair fell on his face, how come Anil was so bereft of an Indian accent all the while *looking so incredibly Indian*??? Must feel weird Stephen thought. Oughtn't language to have a color? Years later, as Stephen sat down to dinner across from an attractive young woman, this thought would come back to nibble at his appetite, eating into his enjoyment of dinner.

Turning his cell phone off he greeted Judy, Ryan and Mike Junior who were already in the conference room. "Well, I am not the one who is late." Stephen said by way of greeting. "We know Anil's supposed to join us as well."

"He went back to his office to bring up a file he thinks we need to refer to for this case, he was here well ahead of us." Judy glanced around the room as she spoke and returned to rest on Stephen. Stephen nodded distractedly, appearing not to notice the implicit reprimand in Judy's voice that he, and not any of the others was late.

Anil returned with some files and they proceeded to discuss the patents they'd filed on behalf of their client. At the end of three hours, Ryan got up to announce he needed more coffee, Stephen sat back in his chair rubbing his neck while Judy excused herself for a "bio-break". Anil looked up from his files at Stephen, "You think we can file these by Thursday?" Stephen looked at his watch, "Can't believe it's almost noon now." Then considering Anil's question "Yes.." He said haltingly, "It's possible." He looked at his calendar on the computer and consulting with his phone said, "If I can clear this meeting tomorrow afternoon in Connecticut, we can do it."

"Let's ask Mary to move the appointments then." Anil said wasting no time and moved quickly to exit the office. After working through a lunch of turkey and Portobello mushroom sandwiches which had air dried as they remained focused heavily on their files and taking very short breaks they finally stopped at 6pm.

Ryan threw down his pen and closed his file. "I need a drink." He got weary looks of agreement from the others. Judy's normally pink face looked even more flushed with the exertion of sitting non-stop bent over files and details. "I don't think I have the energy to come back tonight." Stephen said rubbing his eyes. "Plus I have to prepare a response to the guys from New Jersey and I should send something to the Connecticut guys so they don't kick up a row about canceling tomorrow." Judy looked at everyone. "Let's do dinner, split and find each other in this same room at 8:00 am sharp tomorrow."

Stephen did not engage her look as she glared pointedly at him. "It's tough, but I'll try. I'm a West Coast guy." Then catching her irritated look, "Come on, I was in California for a week!" He shrugged as they walked out. Judy closed the door and locked it slipping the key into her purse. "Guys, actually why don't I beg off dinner, I haven't had dinner with my husband in so long, he will soon forget what I look like. Maybe if I hustle, I can tuck my kiddoes into bed." She walked into the open elevator before anyone could respond.

The men shrugged and waited at the next elevator to ride down. Stephen looked around when they exited, "No sign of Judy, she made her escape very quickly." "Where will it be? Greek food tonight or..." Stephen said looking at his watch, "It's bang in the middle of dinner time, *Pavoni's* will be tough to find a table without reservations, let's do the Greek thing."

"We end up drinking good South American wines in either place!" Anil laughed.

"Agreed. Those Malbecs I tell you I thought I was always a Cab guy." Stephen said. His balding head bobbing into the cab Anil had hailed. They got out and Stephen paid for the cab and stopped to get a receipt as the other two went into the restaurant. Anil held the door open for Stephen. Loosening their ties and pulling off their jackets and draping them over the chair, the men sat down. All three were single. Ryan almost forty, was recently divorced and had a ten year old son who spent weekends with him. Stephen was the oldest one on the team although Judy in her early forties was the project manager for the case they were currently handling. In his mid thirties, Anil was the youngest of the three men. He'd been poached recently from a rival firm by the managing partner and was immediately placed as counsel for the more high profile cases they were handling. Stephen looked at his watch. He was just beginning to unwind. His biological clock was getting used to the confusion it was confronted by with his constant travel between the Coasts and Central Time.

The following week Stephen was back in San Francisco, now his favorite city, although he hadn't 'come out' about it yet. He had spent the previous week working almost constantly with only one night of fun when he had taken Denise out to dinner. Denise looked well. That dress made of some kind of fine silk slimmed her buttocks down, making them appear more shapely than he could remember. Stephen sighed at the memory as he sat on the train in San Francisco remembering his visit with her. He'd taken her to dinner near her apartment in Manhattan. Denise had edged out of their relationship after realizing Stephen treated fidelity issues very casually. Stephen had scrambled to retain contact with her. Denise was on the boards of two non-profits in mid-town Manhattan and was on the boards of museums and foundations. She got invited to high quality events. He needed to keep contact with her. Denise on the other hand remained a friend of Stephen's because he was well read and served as a good short order date for some of the many events she attended as part of her work. He made an erudite companion and people found him engaging, his Ivy league background was something she could flaunt when introducing him to some of the 'old money' people in her network who seemed to forgive you for not being as wealthy as they were if you could sport a fancy college degree. They probably likened it to stepping out of a Lamborghini she thought.

Now sitting on the train in San Francisco headed to the Embarcadero station, Stephen got up with a start realizing he was so lost in his thoughts that he almost forgot to get off. He had made a trip early in the morning all the way to the other end of town to drop off a file for a colleague working at a client's site and was returning on the train as it was the only way to avoid rush hour traffic. He hastily grabbed his large *'lawyer luggage'* as he liked to joke about it and headed out almost knocking over a woman who was also exiting the train. The book she'd been reading on the train fell irretrievably into the gap between the train and the platform and she cried out, "Oh no!" He apologized profusely to her and did a double take when he saw her, *what a face!* She had the face of a Botticelli angel, beautifully shaped and framed by light brown curls with imploring blue eyes. She was apologizing to him. "Oh no! I almost killed you! That was very gross on my part, I am truly sorry. Not to mention you lost your book on my account." Stephen said.

The woman looked down into the gap, she couldn't see her book. She couldn't hold the man responsible for her loss of the book she thought. "No worries. As you can see, I am not so easy to knock over. It's just that it was a signed copy by the author." She said trying to justify her scream.

"That's terrible!" he exclaimed noticing that her delicate face belied a larger body but which somehow didn't completely detract from her beauty. How could she be so neglectful? *How could this angelic woman not cater to keeping her body to match the beauty of her face*? I mean, a cop could potentially write her a ticket for willful negligence. I mean, willfully letting yourself go when you had this *highly redemptive* face? He felt an immediate moral obligation to fix that. "I feel terribly awful about your book." He looked genuinely grieved.

"Listen I am headed to a meeting," He pointed vaguely in the direction of one of the Embarcaderos. "Let me at least buy you the book I just tossed from your hand, I know I can't get it signed by the author or maybe better still I can make it up to you and take you to lunch *and* buy you the book?"

Stephen knew that he perhaps came off a bit too strong with such an upfront request and braced himself for a rebuff. "Hmm, you feel that bad huh?" Olivia laughed embarrassed at this exchange. Stephen stopped on his tracks, *wow! Her teeth! Strung pearls!* And was startled to think the thought was reminiscent of the Big Bad Wolf's words in Little Red Riding Hood. Walking briskly towards the exit he turned around after passing his ticket through and getting out, "I hope that's a yes?" He continued his query, "Where would be a good place do you think?"

Olivia looked up from her phone, "I just got a text from my girl friend, her son is sick and she's going to stay home, looks like our planned lunch is now canceled." "Done!" Stephen exclaimed, ecstatic at the prospect of lunch with the beauty. "Shall we say *Joads' B&B* at 12:30?" He suggested quickly.

Olivia nodded and hopped on to the escalator as he took the stairs. *Joads* was a favorite local breakfast and brunch place. He watched as she went up, her wonderful fuchsia colored scarf had formed an entrancing complement to her matching lips, the picture from the back was far less fetching, certainly one that wouldn't have enticed him into wanting to see the front, but now he knew better. She turned when she reached the top of the stairs and waved self-consciously at Stephen before she disappeared into the crowds by the time he climbed to the top of the stairs.

He was glad she turned to wave goodbye seeing again the reason he'd felt so drawn to her unmistakably striking face. How old could she be? Thirty? Thirty-two. *Maybe* ? He looked at his phone he had a message from Ryan. *"Submitted. We'll know more next week."* He nodded as if Ryan were in front of him and typed in *"yay"* in response before putting his phone away to cross the street.

He reached *Joads' B&B* a good ten minutes earlier and positioned himself a little outside the entrance with a newspaper in hand. He had always thought it a good idea to *'check out'* how the girls arrived. He wanted to observe Olivia's entry. Did other guys look at her as she walked in? Would they be similarly struck by her looks as he had been?

His thoughts hearkened back to a Yale lecture, one of his professors had droned on one gloomy afternoon quoting Nietzche, 'One must pay dearly for immortality; one has to die several times while still alive.' Nietzche must surely have had Stephen in his mind. Stephen had done the whole phoenix resurrecting itself schtick several times now. What with his sixties looming in front of him with a baton in hand, he felt he was in an 'Exit Only' lane on the freeway, except there was no path onward from that Exit. Deeply imaginative and immensely confident with women Stephen wondered if this charming, if, he groped around for the right adjective, 'oversized' opportunity that had presented itself to him on the train could offer a path for him from that Exit Lane. Of course, he had to engineer things the way only he knew how.

"Oh well," he shrugged, he would expense the lunch anyway. It really didn't matter he thought wearily, gosh, these East-West trips did take their toll on one, but he hated sitting alone to eat at a restaurant.

14

Somehow he thought everyone could see a big 'L' for loser hanging on his face when he sat alone.

CHAPTER TWO

At 12:35 Olivia came into view. Stephen moved the paper ever so slightly to see her. She was putting her phone in her bag. She went into the restaurant without looking around, a man walking in, held the door open to let her in, smiling down at her, "After you." Stephen slid in, "Oh there you are!" He said, before Olivia could respond to the man. He held her elbow leading her aside she looked down at his hand wondering what to make of the intimacy of the gesture. *She didn't even know the guy's name, what was she doing here?* She hid her trepidation and smiled slightly. The usher, a young, handsome blond guy came forward to them smiling. Stephen was not short at 5'8 but he hated having to look up at these tall hunky guys who had the advantage of their immense vantage point by *sheer luck of the gene pool draw* he often thought. He looked at Olivia as he spoke, "Table for two?" Stephen piped in before Olivia could speak. "Yes, for two." They were being escorted to a table in the middle of the room flanked by two occupied tables. "Wait a minute." Stephen said, touching the tall guy's elbow. "Can we get something closer to a window do you think?" The waiter looked around, catching sight of one empty table toward the window on his left, "hold on," he said. He went to the computer in the front and returned beaming, "Follow me!" Stephen stepped aside to let Olivia in. "That wasn't hard now was it." Stephen said with an air of accomplishment as Olivia made her way into her seat, pulling it forward. "It's the New Yorker in me" Stephen felt compelled to explain. "The New Yorker in you? Regarding what?" Olivia was baffled.

"Oh I mean, I always get the table I want at a restaurant. The cardinal principle is never to agree to sit at the first place you are offered seating if you think you can do better." "Impressive." Olivia said as her perfectly arched eyebrows rose over smiling eyes. Stephen rubbed his hands before stretching out his right hand.

"I am Stephen Baylor, Yale/Columbia." "Oh" Olivia shook his hand, "I'm Olivia." Not feeling the need to supply her college credentials she chose to look at the menu instead. "What will you have?" Stephen said suddenly feeling the superfluousness of his introduction. "I've eaten here before." Olivia said to soften the fact that she didn't volunteer the name of her college or for that matter, her last name. "It's so convenient. Place is huge, I always find a spot here." Stephen replied opening the menu. "I know what I want, I think it will be the Chinese Chicken Salad and I will ask them to leave out the fried strips of whatever it is they put on top." "I haven't decided yet. It's interesting they have so many dinner entrees for a brunch place." She wrinkled her nose as she considered the menu. "I'll have the 'Joads' Anytime No-mess Spare Ribs." Stephen blinked and fell silent. When the waiter came around he ordered, "The lady will have the Anytime Spare Ribs and I will go with the Chinese Chicken Salad." The waiter took their menus back as he gave Olivia a thumbs up, "That's the all time favorite here." "Mine too!" Olivia smiled happily. "So what were you reading that I so rudely tossed from your hands this morning?" "Oh well, it was an older Martha Bates novel." "Hmm, my parents are big fans of hers. Can't recall if I read any of her books. I may have, years ago."

"This one was one of her earlier novels that I hadn't read before." "I am so sorry for tossing it from your hands, a Martha Bates signed novel, I mean, that borders on criminal negligence." His hyperbolic statement of regret elicited a pearly laugh from her. "What do you do?" Olivia was mildly curious about him. The man was buying her lunch.

"Oh well, where do I begin? I..." he closed his eyes in thought and blurted out all at once. "Well I'm a lawyer." "Why do you sound like you are confessing to a crime?" Olivia laughed. "That's funny! You know, no one's ever said that to me. That's really funny." He laughed looking at the light reflecting in her hair.

"I went to UC Davis for my undergrad." Olivia said, feeling churlish for being sarcastic. "Oh, you are a California girl through and through then?" "I guess so, born and raised in Carmel."

"Interesting." Stephen muttered distractedly. Carmel, he thought, you had to have money to live in Carmel. "Did you like UC Davis?" "Loved it! It was great fun. I am still good friends with a ton of my college mates."

"That's great! I wish I could say the same. You know. My career. I travel so much. You are a lucky girl! I mean, lucky most times I guess, just not this morning when I caused you to lose your signed copy of Martha Bates' novel, that was terrible!" Olivia wondered why Stephen felt the need to exclaim so much. "Don't know about lucky but I know I am happy." She responded. "I am guessing you are not from California?" She twirled the stem of her water glass.

"No. I am a New Yorker!" Olivia felt he would have embellished it with color pens and exclamation points had he been writing that instead of saying it. The waiter brought their food and Stephen was disappointed he didn't get to say it with the full flourish he had intended.

Olivia spread her napkin on her lap and dug into the ribs with care and concentration. She wondered if Stephen had children, it would be reasonable to expect him to have children around her age, feeling she could well be his daughter.

Stephen noticed Olivia's plump white hands holding the knife and fork firmly cutting into the meat. No ring on her finger. She seemed like such a nice, average girl, but with potential, he thought emphatically, looking again at her chiseled features and fine teeth. How could she let herself go like that? The curve of her lower lip was so defined, inviting a finger to run along its definition. He knew it wasn't a trick of clever make-up artistry. Women these days could do anything he thought, she didn't seem like the kind to have too much patience for wearing make up.

Olivia looked up from her meal. "This is so good!" He nodded approvingly, "least I could do."

She was reminded suddenly as to why she was here, eating lunch with a perfect stranger and set her knife and fork down. "Oh, that was nothing, if I were to get free lunches each time I got jostled in the crowd, I would never have to work again! All my lunches would be paid for." She laughed and her smile broke the clouds of reserve beginning to crowd Stephen's mind. God, she *is* uncommonly pretty he thought.

"Do you have family in the Bay Area?" he asked, suddenly curious to know more about this almost perfect creature. Just the fullness and roundness of her hips, just a tad too round, from where he sat, he could feel the extra rolls growing on her waist as she tucked into her meal with concentration. Man, she didn't need that lunch, did no one ever tell her how fatal it was to her chances to have this excess? Who knew? She could be completely unattached for all her beauty because of this propensity for plumpness she clearly seemed to have.

She licked her lips daintily and dabbed at her mouth with the napkin before sitting back in her chair with a sigh, "Well, my mother is Martha Bates, that signed copy was one she gave me when I was heading to college, I..." She never got to finish what she had to say.

Stephen dropped his fork, "Get out of here!" He stood up agitatedly, "You are the daughter of Martha Bates?!" Olivia had gone and done it, she'd knocked him down with a feather! Something she had always wondered about. Here was this man, apparently enjoying his salad, now about to lose his sense of gravity.

"Sit down!" She urged, looking self-consciously around her. "Do you have *any* idea of the celebrity you are!" He cried agitatedly.

"How does my mother being a best selling author make me a celebrity?" She had never willingly told people she was her mother's daughter unless the occasion called for it, feeling neither the need to hide the fact nor expose it without good reason.

Stephen was clearly transported. Did she have any idea what this could mean for *him*? I mean, he thought, all those New York parties I could take her to, essentially *flaunt* her at. "Your mother is one of the more well known authors of the twentieth century in the entire English speaking world!"

He enunciated his words as if he was talking to a child explaining to Olivia the dire consequences of a traffic ticket or some such transgression. On the other hand his thoughts were away in New York, with his colleagues. He could be a dark horse and say nothing of her parental details until he had all the guys crowd around her for her looks and charm and then slowly knock them over with this news. *Absolutely knock them over*. The potential for drama in it enthralled and inspired him. The conversations spun dizzyingly in his head. This was the closest he'd come to this level of celebrity. Four hundred or more years ago it would be like hanging out with Shakespeare's daughter for heaven's sake! He could not afford to screw this up. He intended to handle this correctly. When the waiter came around again, he asked for the dessert menu.

"Oh no!" Olivia exclaimed, "I don't think I can squeeze in another spoon of anything more." "A sorry is not a sorry unless you sweeten it with a fine dessert." He asserted commandingly. His entire demeanor had transformed from hesitant courtship to being exuberantly engaging. He asked the waiter authoritatively, "What is the absolute best dessert you have on your menu?" "Well, it's a toss up between our Cinnamon Panna Cotta and the Warm Chocolate Cake drizzled with rum and topped with our homemade pure Vanilla ice cream." "We don't like toss ups, now do we?" He winked conspiratorially at Olivia who smiled shaking her head, she couldn't think of eating any more. She looked down at her hands in her lap. But Stephen was on a high. Unstoppable, "We'll get both. And, can you make sure to get me a large decaf please? Anything for you to drink Olivia?" She looked resignedly at him, "I am awfully full but if I am going to have to eat dessert, I'll probably ask for an espresso so I don't fall asleep at my desk." The waiter left with the menus.

She straightened up in her chair and said, "I didn't need the dessert maybe." "Oh just eat a little to celebrate our coming together. My parents are great fans of your mother's works. I've read a couple, but don't ask me which ones it's been a while. All I can recall is that I read them in quick succession. They are quite contagious!" She blinked at the *'coming together'* part. "Are you always very busy?" She queried suddenly, curious that he was extending his lunch hour so. "Ha!" he laughed. "I am a New York lawyer. You don't know New York lawyers, they are a different breed than any other." "How so?" she questioned. "Well, passing the New York bar is a trip in and of itself you know and then, just dealing with so much talent, that's it! That's just it! It's the most densely talented place on the planet. I mean, you gotta love it! New York!" She felt he should be wearing the flag of New York on him somehow, a lapel pin maybe? "My mother visited New York often when I was young but she didn't stay too long. She always told me she wanted to be back home."

"As I recall, doesn't Martha Bates have two children?" Stephen asked her. "Yes, my older brother. He's on the opposite coast, he teaches at Harvard." "Oh my!" Stephen couldn't believe his luck. Talk about deep encounters he thought. "And you are not married yet I assume?" He had to ask her that, he'd been meaning to ask her that since he saw her but now it was imperative that she not be committed to anyone. The absence of the ring on her finger wasn't sufficient proof that she wasn't married. Oh yes, he'd run into that one before, this utterly comely half Asian and half whatever girl, silken smooth like chiffon chocolate cake. They had been in the middle of an intense conversation about the rotten luck they'd had with finding cabs in the past week due to the conference at Moscone Center. They were seated in the foyer of the hotel he was staying in. He presumed she was there for the conference and just as he decided to move closer to her and edged forward her husband came by and kissed her full on the mouth apologizing for taking so much time. Some girls just didn't wear any rings at all. He clearly saw the potential in Olivia and knew exactly how to go about working on fixing her, her, he searched for the right word, her one *'drawback' shortcoming, over-endowdness? handicap?* Could he think that without making it seem like it was a disability?

"No, I am not. Broke off my engagement last month." Stephen fought hard to control his delight. With more restraint than he ever thought he possessed, he mumbled, "I'm awfully sorry to hear that, what a complete bag of a fellow would break up with one of the most charming women in San Francisco."

"Oh no" Olivia butt into his eloquent defense of her, "*I* broke it off. I couldn't see it working out. Markus has too many passions, his music, his DJ stuff, his friends dropping in at all hours, too many." Stephen thought of all these things twenty- somethings were obsessed with.

"It must be comforting not to be in my age group any more... I mean" She continued, "I mean, it must be nice not to have to worry about this dating business, finding your niche with a guy, reinventing yourself and all that jazz. My parents are both single adults but they don't seem to go around with aching hearts."

"That's right your parents are divorced aren't they? Where do they live?" "Locally." She answered briefly. Wondering at her uncharacteristic ebullience.

She was obliquely curious of Stephen's marital status. Stephen saw that she was referring to his age, his face flushed and he cleared his throat emphatically before looking around gravely. "Well, my last girl friend was younger than you are." His voice came out defiant and peevish at her assumption that he was perhaps too old to be in the dating game. It was Olivia's turn to flush with embarrassment now.

CHAPTER THREE

Among the many rules Stephen operated under, it was always to tell a current prospect that his 'most recent' or 'almost current' girl friend was in her twenties, was 5' 5" tall, weighed a little over eighty pounds and was phenomenally talented. It wasn't an exaggeration.

Sharing this tidbit of information was the surest way for a girl to start second guessing all her plusses right there, right away. It was an arresting image that girls were awestruck by. They conjured up a picture of a leggy blonde or brunette with feather light accoutrements to match her person, wafting down a hallway propelled by the wind. The only reason they found this scenario quasi possible was because of the way Stephen pitched his undeniably impressive Ivy studded resume, his sophisticated manner and his dogged persistence to get that impossible dream of a woman into bed.

Stephen had a romantic and possessive relationship

with New York to which he alternated between being a lover and a parent, sometimes feeling like he'd birthed the streets of Manhattan. He gave off an air of a seasoned Maitre 'D at an established restaurant, suave, assured, better read than his clientele, like butlers in royal English households, all knowing and starchy. New York was that venerated an establishment for him, functioning under his discerning eye. He had also developed this apparent ease with social situations, his incessant compliments that erased any doubts his unsuspecting guest could potentially be harboring about his intent, he was just a suave guy who got his way because he was so impeccably credentialed.

It wasn't that he picked indiscriminate, needy women, quite the opposite. Norma, one of the women he was 'seeing' was a bookstore clerk and a high order intellectual. She was recently being interviewed to submit some of her writings on Proust to a European literary magazine. She was clearly an intelligent, if humbly paid, woman who was attracted to Stephen. She approached him first in the bookstore she worked at asking him if he needed help finding anything. She was flattered by his attentive response to her she'd always considered herself the opposite of glamorous and was smitten by the fact that Stephen was smitten by her. She had never paused to examine whether his attentions were constant, whether he was treating her frivolously. She was happy to have this part-time, semi-permanent, ad hoc set up they had developed. It suited her just fine.

Emma Joy, his other 'Denver Distraction' as he put it, was nobody's fool either. Savvy, street smart, she knew the value of being this close to a topnotch lawyer. She had dabbled in trying out various businesses, from patented exercise videos to protein infused energy drinks. It would be imperative for her to obtain a lawyer at some point when she did launch her products into the market. Stephen and his *fancy schmancy* law firm would come handy some day, she was sure of that. Meanwhile, it felt good not to have to worry about pitching in at pricey restaurants. Stephen never expected his girl to do that. He always picked up the tab in willing anticipation of the night ahead.

The waiter arrived with their desserts cutting into Stephen's reverie.

"You can't be serious!" She gasped looking at the portions. At least she's shocked Stephen thought feeling redemption was possible. He watched as Olivia tasted a little of his dessert and then some of hers. "Why did you choose to go to UC Davis, I mean you being Martha Bates' daughter and all and with your brother teaching at Harvard."

She blinked at the sudden change in subject, "Why ever not?" She replied incredulously. "I loved Davis. I had other choices perhaps but I went there because my high school boyfriend got into Davis too, he was planning to be a doctor."

"And is he?" Stephen asked. He needed to know everything about her. The casual manner in which she seemed to treat her celebrity piqued his curiosity about her even more.

"He is now. He started dating a medical student immediately after we broke up and five years later they got married. But we are still good friends, I see them fairly often when the old gang gets together." She continued in a defensive tone about her college.

"So were you a spoilt babe growing up?" He smiled cajolingly at her. An unpleasant ripple ran through her at the term *'babe'* but she said nothing for a few moments. "Not really. I loved to read and had just one best friend all through elementary and middle school so, no. I was always the same to my small circle of friends." Her tone was deliberately flat and matter of fact. She wanted to debunk any theories he had of her being some kind of princess. She had felt little impact being her mother's daughter. Aside from some social and life style givens she didn't feel particularly sidelined for either pleasure or pain any more so than most of her friends.

Barring her one horrific childhood experience that she shoved back in like an old, embarrassing sock full of holes, one she shuddered to bring to the fore of her consciousness, possibly her scariest memory, she hurriedly moved past that thought, barring that however, she had been buffeted by the same vicissitudes as most people born into privilege and loving families. Yes, her heart had been broken several times. When all four of five girls who had tried out were accepted into the cheer leading squad and she had to walk away with a brave smile, that hadn't been easy, especially when she managed to see Amanda's smirkful wink at her friends on Olivia's disqualification, she had rolled her eyes signaling with her hands that Olivia was too fat for the team. Those were only some from her selection of heart breaking moments. She knew she was no 'spoilt babe' a lot of what she had didn't come easily to her. She had paid squarely for it she thought.

Stephen didn't want to hit the wrong notes with Olivia, maybe she was an upright and serious girl and dubbing her a 'spoilt babe' wasn't the best way to win her over, he had sensed her unease settling in.

He thought for a moment, "Did you know that San Francisco was originally going to be called Yerba Buena?" She furrowed her brow, "There's a whole Yerba Buena neighborhood not far from here, but no, I didn't know that." "Do you know what it means?" Stephen loved telling San Franciscans basic facts about the city they lived in that they ought to know, she shook her head ruefully. "It means Good Weed." She laughed,

"That would have been so apt! What ever caused them to christen it San Francisco instead? We have too many Sans around here, San Mateo, San Jose, San Fernando, Yerba Buena would have singled the city out, like Carmel, it would have given it an even more distinctive personality perhaps."

"I don't know about that!" Stephen exclaimed laughing, glad he was able to reconnect with her and engage her, for a moment he thought he'd lost her. "It would have given people license to never get off the weed perhaps!" She shrugged as she walked ahead of him.

As they exited the hotel, Stephen handed Olivia his business card. "We have to do this again soon. I am in San Francisco more than twice a month." She looked at his card, "Jones & Boyle, do they have a branch in San Francisco?" She vaguely recalled seeing ads in magazines or on TV or something.

Stephen explained patiently, "Yes. They are the largest law firm in North America." He looked at her face to see the effect this had on her. She nodded raising her eyebrows slightly, acquiescing his unspoken request that she be impressed. "I need to get back to work."

CHAPTER FOUR

Stephen suddenly realized she could be gone now and it was possible he would never find her again. He almost panicked at the thought. His reverie was about to end in oblivion. He quickly grabbed another card from his wallet, "Could you write your number here please?" She looked at the card as she put her scarf into her purse and made to depart. "Okay then."

He came across and held her lightly by the shoulders she edged away instinctively at the intimacy, "My, what a pretty girl!" blushing at his effusive compliment, Stephen was assessing her again, she was probably 5'4 he thought and noticed how his arm had to stretch across to encircle her. Typically he liked his girls small enough to enable his hand to hang around the hollowness that a nicely curved waistline would allow. The girls were perfect when his hand slid across their waists effortlessly, not touching any flesh but resting lightly on the hipbone. He had tested that one out many, many times. It was a precise way to tell if someone was perfectly apportioned. In Stephen's mind he had several formulas he'd come up with to *'measure'* the date-worthiness of a girl. He felt he pretty much had a foolproof theory that had emerged as a result.

Olivia was a *'fixable'* problem. People like Olivia didn't just cross your path every day. Yes, she didn't go to Harvard, but she didn't need to. People of her ilk didn't need to be embellished with a Harvard degree. In his state of frenzied anticipation and plotting he saw as clearly as the nose on his face that Harvard could use the embellishment of having her. He kept telling himself that throughout the lunch as he watched her unselfconsciously tuck into her food without regret or apology. He knew in New York people familiar with him would keel over and die if they saw him order dessert, it would be tantamount to robbing a bank at gunpoint.

He did it only to extend the conversation with her, now how was the poor dear going to shave off all those calories? She needed his help without question. He could well be her savior. So much could be managed, but he first had to find a way to kick this door open, there was no way he was going to let her slip away.

Stephen's thoughts turned to Sandra, his girl from many years ago in Denver and even as her outstandingly slim figure came into his mind as a taunt to his current interest, he brushed the thought away. Sandra had been an aspiring opera singer. She'd never make it in his opinion, not because she lacked talent, she had plenty of that but who said success in the world of arts and letters had anything to do with talent he thought bitterly, having been an aspiring author almost all his adult life and having nothing published to show for it, he was testament to the fact that talent had nothing to do with success. Sandra just wouldn't get those all-important career breaks. The amount of time it took to market your work! Phew! He shook his head in despair.

Sandra had however been his first 'success' story. He'd met her at a mutual friend's home, had found her comely and the most attractive girl in the room and decided she had potential, her rotund looks notwithstanding. He'd taken her back to his apartment that night and had embarked on a 'Sandra Slimming' mission for the next few months. Both of them jogged, developed a common love for fresh fruit and meals that excluded entirely foods from a can or from a freezer and within six months or so Sandra had that edgy good looking face with a tautness of skin that had also resulted in a tightness in her manner. She soon tired of Stephen and started dating one of the theatre managers. It was possible, was all *that* experience was trying to tell Stephen.

Olivia was walking out of the restaurant with his card in her hand. Stephen knew he was hopelessly late but he had the grandest excuse, he was certain. Imagine walking into Fenton's office and telling him he'd just met up with an old pal, actually Martha Bates' daughter and was held up talking to her. How about that! He thought.

He paused outside the restaurant and put his hand on her arm gently. "Olivia, I did cause you to lose your book, I need to do more than buy you one lame lunch. How do I get to stay in touch with you?" Olivia tried to hide her confusion, what was he after she thought perplexed. She needed to hurry back to her desk but she succumbed to his query, to the pale blue eyes imploring her and she wrote her number down thinking he couldn't possibly be interested in her as a potential date, the thought seemed ludicrous! Yes, his watery blue eyes had an intensity that belied their wateriness and the confidence he sought to exude seemed a little too forceful but, she shrugged, at least she had the option to ignore the phone calls should she feel like it, she thought.

With mixed feelings, she wrote her work number down on his card and returned it to him. "I head this way," she pointed away from the water to her left.

He had to scramble and turning in the other direction

fled to keep his appointment with Fenton knowing he wouldn't make much progress if he ambled along beside her. He started to sprint in an attempt to melt away the calories piled on at lunch. *My oh my! How could people be so unthinking!* Olivia's face flashed in front of him, and how pretty!

Always interested in the appropriateness of diction, which he attributed to being a New York lawyer, he thought he didn't know any other woman who could be called pretty more justifiably than Olivia. Of course he wasn't going to wait for her to call him, *he* would call her. He stopped sprinting and paused to look at her card, at the progress she was going to make getting back to her office, he figured he would beat her to it and leave her a message to get back to. What if she dismissed him from her thoughts? He needed to get her to continue to think of him.

Strategy was all-important in securing someone as eminently *'catch-worthy'* as Olivia. Were all the men in San Francisco blind or just stupid he wondered. Maybe a good number of them were gay, he shook his head in continued bafflement trying to find answers to Olivia's singleness. The person who could snare this prize opportunity that Olivia clearly could be transformed into had to be heavily credentialed, have an imagination, be suave and comfortable with women and know them inside out, it required a person of some intellectual heft and fiber, it required him, Stephen was convinced of that.

CHAPTER FIVE

When Olivia returned to her office, she had a string of voice mail messages. She played them in order and paused briefly to hear a remotely familiar voice, huh, this Stephen guy, he'd called her already?! Pretty crazy, she thought. She pressed save and went on to the more pressing messages. Yes, her boss was her mother's attorney's friend but that had only allowed her résumé to get viewing time. She did go through grueling interviews and a nail biting wait for more than two months before she was told the job was hers. She never abused that connection, never missing a chance to prove her mettle. Maybe her engagement with Markus would not have broken off if she hadn't been so glued to her job responsibilities.

The next morning as she sat in her office with her marketing assistant, the ever witty and fun Robert standing next to her pouring over the new brochure he was working on, she got a phone call from Stephen, she picked up the phone glancing at the number on the monitor absent mindedly. She paused and held the phone away from her ear twisting her mouth in a grimace she capped the mouthpiece of the phone, "Can't believe I picked it up!" she mouthed to Robert who looked at her and said, "do you want me to come back?" he whispered. "No, this should be quick, bear with me." She whispered back holding her hand over the mouthpiece, she frowned into the phone.

"Hello, hello." Stephen's voice on the other end was insistent. She took a deep breath and finally said "hello?" inquiringly into the phone, pretending not to recognize his voice. "It's Stephen Baylor! Attorney, Yale, Columbia! Remember!" "Huh, how could I forget!" Olivia's veiled sarcastic voice was lost on him. "Listen, I have tickets to the San Francisco Symphony, it's a Mahler concert tonight."

"And?" Olivia asked. "I'd like you to come!" Gosh he didn't waste any time, so he was making a play for her? She wasn't sure how he figured she would be even remotely interested. Was it something she'd said at lunch? Wasn't he way too old for her? She thought quickly. Markus was supposed to drop in tonight to pick up his last bit of luggage and his guitar. She wondered if it wouldn't be a good idea to just be out of the house when Markus showed up. It could save both her and Markus some awkwardness plus he still had a key to her place so he would let himself in to reclaim his possessions.

"What time is it?" She asked aware that Robert was presumably looking at the draft but could potentially be listening to her conversation. "I'll pick you up at 6:30 pm, we can get a bite to eat after."

"No, I can't eat anything after, I'll grab some soup before" She said, realizing she'd now agreed to go with him. Well, she told herself, just the symphony and out. No, no, no dropping her off or anything, she'd take the cab. "I'll get a cab, no problem. See you there, here's my number, 212..." Of course, she thought as she scribbled it down, he'd have a 212 area code, New Yorker that he was.

She returned her attention to Robert who couldn't resist asking, "Plans tonight?" "Seems so," Olivia murmured focusing on the edits he had made, she crossed out one of the passages, inserted a line, changed the fonts on the introductory paragraph and drew a red line through the last paragraph. "I think it's very eloquent to stop with that line, any more is overkill."

"Okay, I'll fix that." Robert sighed and took the documents with him. Olivia brushed her hair in the bathroom at the end of the day. She glanced at her watch and saw that she had another half hour. Digging into her purse, she emerged with a hair clip and scooped her hair in one big swirl on one side, a colleague exiting one of the stalls in the bathroom exclaimed as she washed her hands, "Hmm *nice*!!" Olivia smiled her thank you and waved, holding the clip in her with her teeth, unable to speak. She slid her hair into the clip, put on some lipstick and glancing at herself one last time, walked out. Her fuchsia colored scarf now acting as a shawl lending an air of formality, it'll have to do she thought given she'd not had any notice regarding this. She hadn't dressed up.

She rode the elevator down, grabbed the San Francisco Chronicle and sat in the coffee shop below with a cup of soup and some buttered bread before she headed out to find a taxi to take her to the symphony. She checked her text message from Markus, 'will be picking up my stuff around 9pm.'

'Okay, I'm out at an event.' She responded and settled back in the cab. She found Stephen waiting below at the entrance of Symphony Hall. He hurried forward as soon as he saw her and made to give her a hug, she retrieved herself from it quickly laughing shyly. "Hmm, did you get prettier? I didn't think it was possible. I like that thing holding your hair up."

She laughed, "You mean the hair clip? It's a birthday gift from Aunt Connie, she said it was her life saver clip when she had to look nice in an emergency."

42

"Boy, was she someone with good taste?" He gushed. "I just keep it handy, it's an easy fix for long hair."

He looked attentively at her, really pretty face he thought. It would look so much more chiseled and the contours would emerge more beautifully once he helped her 'tone it down,' he evaluated. His eyes wandered over the rest of her, the unnecessary set of bulges. Who was crazy enough to call them *'love handles?'* Were they nuts? Why confuse the poor women into thinking it was something romantic, these, these doughy folds?! They *HAD* to go he thought barely stopping himself from shaking his head in disapproval.

Clueless of his scrutiny, Olivia paused to look at the signs announcing future concerts with Michael Tilson Thomas conducting Appalachian Spring. She was hoping to remember to get tickets so she could take her dad to the concert for his birthday, he would enjoy that.

She tripped on the final step and was steadied by a man escorting a woman up the stairs, "Thank you!" Olivia muttered and nodded to the couple. "Enjoy the concert dear." The man's wife whispered loudly to her husband, "hmm, look at that hair,

I'm getting mine fixed next week too!" She said patting her hair as she smiled at her husband.

Stephen immediately pounced into the empty space. "Sorry, I was trying to turn off my phone, I sometimes forget and can embarrass myself in theatres and other events." He said largely. He guided her by the elbow toward their seats, "Did you hear what that woman said? See, even women fall for you." He said taking his cue from what he overheard of the woman's comment.

"Oh well." Olivia sighed. She liked how she looked, she thought most people seemed to like how she looked but how she looked had not been a preoccupation with her, nor for that matter, with the men who had dated her. Markus had always said he'd loved her *"easy, uncomplicated charm."* Olivia reveled in the comfort of that thought.

After the concert Stephen insisted on getting a cab and dropping her off but she put her foot down, "I have no idea which direction you are headed but my drive is clear up the hill and I don't want to take you out of your way."

"You sure?" Stephen asked her feebly, unsure how to handle this display of obstinacy.

She nodded firmly. He called a cab and she slid into the seat and waved a goodbye quickly before rolling up her window to give the driver her address so Stephen was out of earshot.

Digging his hands into his pocket, Stephen decided he was going to walk the short distance to his hotel. So, the lady didn't appreciate his trying to put his hand over hers at the concert. She had been quite engrossed in watching the performance and was clearly enjoying herself. He had felt an instinctive urge to touch her hand to commemorate a shared pleasure for the music, like butter on bread, just seemed to call for it. When Olivia realized her hand was held captive in his, she pulled away sitting forward in her seat. She sat that way through to the end of the performance. She was quite learned in the arts he reckoned. Little surprise that she should be given her background, he told himself approvingly, he'd detected that certain something hadn't he?

He wondered how he would move this to the next level. He had to leave for New York tomorrow and he felt like he hadn't made the headway he was aiming to prior to his leaving.

Usually the gestation period between taking a woman out to a restaurant and getting her into bed was a matter of hours if he put his mind to it. No, he was no roué, but he liked to have sex. Raise your hands in honesty men, if you think you don't like sex, he often queried to an imaginary group of gathered men who would reflect on Stephen's ways with women. There was too little time to see her again before leaving. He wondered if it would be trying too hard if he sent her flowers at work, but he didn't even know her work address. All he had was her office phone number. She had not given him her cell phone number. He had no way of finding her email address. He started to think, hmm, she worked for a large financial services firm, or so it appeared in the conversation they'd exchanged. She hadn't used the word 'large' but he figured smaller firms didn't normally have too many layers of employees, large firms sand bagged and used excess resources when the business tide flowed, making their employees do internal work when outside work ebbed and redeployed them for client work when things got hectic. That's how things were with a lot of his corporate clients not to mention at his firm.

He dialed her number again knowing she wouldn't be at her desk to pick it up, he reached her recorded greeting. "Hi this is Olivia, please leave me a message." Huh, he thought. No mention of what company you'd dialed or anything in her greeting. He pressed '0' for the operator. The operator's nasal male voice was also a recording, "Thank you for calling 'Stahlberg Financial'. Stephen hung up. *Thank you! Thank you!* For making me so smart he thought and almost skipped along. He knew where she worked. He would figure out a way to send her an email. The next morning he called Stahlberg Financial, "Hello!" he greeted the operator who answered the phone, "Listen, I am trying to get some information on the new tax law recommendations you folks put out the other day."

"Who did you need to speak with sir?"

Stephen licked his lips, digging the phone closer to his head, "Well, I was trying to reach Mark Goodberg." The public relations article he'd seen online mentioned him as the resident tax expert. "How do I send him an email do you know?" "Well sir, I can put you through to his assistant and she can help you further."

"Well, I am not too happy that Mark hasn't responded to me you know." His voice came through angrily when the secretary's voice answered. "Sir, what email address are you using? It's not like Mr. Goodberg not to respond." The woman's voice was only slightly laced with concern, the arrogance of support staff at these large firms he thought indignantly, they took care to show they didn't care. Careful not to reveal his irritation in his tone, he said, "Well, I have," he hesitated and then said, "mark.goodberg@stahlbergfinancial.com." "That should be right sir," the woman confirmed. "Let me try him again then, thank you very much for your help!" He hung up. It could have been tricky if he'd gotten the email convention wrong.

So now it would be, Olivia.bates@stahlbergfinancial.com He looked at his watch and was pretty certain he needed to get his butt to the airport soon. He'd checked out of his hotel skipping breakfast, taking a large black coffee on the go instead. He was so intent on getting it right with Olivia that he quickly became absorbed into thinking of his concurrent relationships.

Holding his head down for a minute he tried to focus and not think of Denise back in New York. He'd agreed to go to the opening of a newly remodeled wing at the museum in Queens on Friday night. He'd probably ask her out to dinner after that if nothing more interesting came up. The space around her eyes was revealing those infamous crows feet. The decline had begun. He recalled that her elbows were getting dimpled, pudgy mounds around the point of the elbow. At one point in the evening he counted three distinct dimples, hmmm, he thought, older *and* whatever. **Double jeopardy.**

There *was* a reason why he was so selective about his women and why they should preferably be below thirty. The liability was greater when they got older.

He remembered sitting through a lecture in a Psychology class and the professor was lecturing about those decades that people's lives were split into; the first decade, one of insouciance, the second of abandon, the third of ambition and anxiety, the fourth of diligence, the fifth of relative calm, the sixth of complications due to health, the seventh decade was mostly spent getting prepared for the eighth, if it came to that and the eighth, staring out of the window contemplating oblivion. Yes, he knew how that map worked. Far as he was concerned, a younger woman would draw his decades in the reverse direction, force him back to his youth. He would get to tread twice on those same steps as before with pulsating and exciting youth beside him and his expert counsel which would help the ladies skirt those annoying pitfalls and dangers that they could otherwise encounter without the vigilant Stephen guiding them by their young, smooth elbows.

His Denver Distractions were different. Emma Joy was a personal trainer at the local gym. She'd done other jobs, waitressing, dog walking, etc. She had broken up with her boyfriend a few months after meeting Stephen but didn't know where she stood with Stephen. He seemed obsessed with her physical training and exercise tips. Her abs and buttocks were TV commercial quality. Stephen called her Joy, because she gave him so much joy he told her as she laughed merrily. Of course he did end up picking up the tab at some fancy restaurants in downtown that she had previously worked at. She found it fun to be waited on at these places although she recognized none of the waiters and the old fart of a Maitre d' only vaguely seemed to have recognized her and wouldn't let on even if he did.

Heads did turn when he walked into a restaurant with Emma Joy. God knows where she shopped but she could look spiffy on a dime. Her long earrings dangling below her swept up auburn hair, that smashing smile that transformed her face and her oh so long legs. But Stephen knew Emma Joy was not someone who would be with him for the long haul. She was like him in some respects, distracted by attentive males that she ran into frequently. But it was so grand to hold her close in bed and feel a sense of possession of that fabulous body, however temporarily.

And then of course there was Norma, who was a little older than Emma Joy at thirty one years old but was stimulating with all the reading she did and her avid recounting of experiences with customers, forcing Stephen to listen to passages she'd selected to read aloud to him with zeal. Her eyes shone brightly as she read and her voice had a slight quiver. If Norma had been a little more ambitious and less content to be just a bookstore clerk, she would have been his big time gal, he often thought ruefully at such times. Norma had arrived at her Mecca in bookstore.

She was so proud of it she acted like it was her home and customers there were guests come to visit. She all but stopped at serving tea there. She didn't seem to care for the more high-end restaurants in Denver, she was happy to grab a pizza and sit in his room to watch a movie after they'd made love. He found her attractive and eminently satisfying in bed. She somehow managed not to gain any weight at all, remaining reed thin, giving her an air of undernourished vulnerability that he found attractive. It was likely the poor girl didn't eat much because she saved even on food.

Sometimes however he thought she smelled too much of the bookstore, he had untangled a cobweb from her hair once. "I was dusting the top shelf in Psychology today and maybe caught something!" she had laughed self- consciously. She did regale him with stories of customers and the strange behavior of bookstore browsers. It took all sorts she said, her sense of humor and the things she found funny enough to recount as well as always adding a literary twist to her anecdotes appealed to Stephen's own literary leanings. Norma was an attractive and scholarly diversion from his sometimes impossibly long workdays when there were times he barely saw the light of day. If only her whole demeanor weren't so *non-descript!* These women weren't that rare, were they? I mean, he thought, she was attractive, engaging and employed but please, how could you have your life's goal be to be a shop girl even if it was at a famed bookstore?

He often got in to work early in the morning and emerged late evening from a ragged day of negotiating contracts, going over details on the intellectual property picket fences he put up for his clients, scanning over the work of the assistant attorneys to ensure they weren't being sloppy. He was meticulous in his work realizing very early on that sloppiness in that regard could be lethal to his success. Sloppiness could endanger so much, all the things he prized so dearly; his social life, he assumed everyone was envious of his personal life, always holding a svelte twenty something year old on his arm. He was the person who had the most to share at any group discussion the best connoisseur of wine and women especially when the table happened to comprise only of men.

But Norma on the other hand seemed to celebrate her hourly wage existence; she was the least ambitious person he'd met. She loved to punch in at 10 in the morning, punch out at 8 pm, most days. On weekends she closed the store, so she worked from noon until 10pm. She usually met him for a drink afterward in his small flat in downtown Denver. But he shook his head ruefully when he thought of her, she just lacked social buoyancy that girl, yes, that was the word, *that* was her Achilles' heel. Not too many would concur with Stephen. Norma's male co- workers and guys who frequented the store found Norma profoundly attractive, the girl just didn't seem to be much inclined to explore beyond Stephen and remained true to her 'not so steady yet somewhat calm and undemanding' relationship with him.

With Emma Joy he had to be careful, she would scoff

at his somewhat humble digs, well at least by what he'd led her to believe, she would have been right in expecting that he lived in more lavish quarters. She was his more expensive proposition and got to meet him in hotels, when he was able to write a hotel stay off as a business expense.

His clients didn't need to know his home base was in Denver, he spent less than fifty percent of his time here, so he wasn't legally obligated to declaring anything. For that matter, he spent about thirty percent of his time in each of the big metros; New York, Denver and more recently San Francisco.

He spent the remaining ten percent traveling and up in the air in "No man's land" as he liked to joke with his secretary Shawna, a large black lady with a brilliant white smile who kept colorful pictures of her grand kids on her desk. Shawna kept track of his travel and expenses. He never forgot to get Shawna a handsome gift at Christmas. He would be dead without her he knew that for a fact. Shawna had developed a big tolerance for small egos. She'd been with the firm for close to thirty years now, her time with Stephen coming on to seven years. She served three of the partners on the floor, Stephen was actually the least demanding and the most together, she thought. The other guys were a shambles, she ended up talking to their wives about everything, children's game schedules, food allergies, man, she had her own stuff to keep track of. Her son depended on her far too much having fathered three children in quick succession and driving a UPS delivery truck meant she picked up the youngest from daycare after work. Her daughter-in-law worked in the finance unit of a department store, a reticent, skinny young woman who kept mostly to herself.

Shawna actually enjoyed working for Stephen. He had no wife she was forced to talk to. She appreciated the thoughtful and generous gifts he gave her at Christmas. Last year she took her whole family, her son, his wife and the three grandkids to an all expenses paid dinner at O'Learys! *Come on, who could afford O'Learys these days?!* They had loved it. Stephen had arranged it with the restaurant so the family could eat dinner and the manager of the restaurant had his credit card details to charge the dinner to, including the tip.

She thought of the greeting card at Christmas, *"Merry Christmas Shawna my love! Here's wishing you a wonderful dinner any time you choose within the next four to five weeks with your entire family! It's on Pa Stephen!"* She had risen from her seat to envelope him in a hug and he felt immediately gratified by her exuberance. Some extravagant gifts were so worth it he thought happily. On Administrative Assistant appreciation day, he was sure to send her flowers with a stuffed toy included so she could give it to one of her grand kids. She did love Stephen, no question. He was a son of a gun with the girls, but that was not her business. She refused to be his moral meter like how some of the others felt about the partners around here, most of the partners were male, there were a total of nine female partners in the entire firm. She knew the other secretaries gossiped about Stephen, especially after company Christmas parties, when he'd never brought the same girl to two successive Christmas parties yet.

Shawna laughed at the jokes but never said anything. He was a bachelor going around with younger women. In her opinion at least he was honest about his preferences, not like some of these other schmucks who purportedly had long 'loving' marriages with their wives of twenty or more years only to have sleazy goings on, on the side. She knew that was more often the case than not. But the thing Shawna liked most about Stephen was how direct and transparent his expenses were. With few questions, she got all the clarification she needed. No sirree, Shawna was not going to just sit there and say bad things about Stephen, he was a good guy in her book and not the least because he got her nice presents, Shawna could abide by womanizers, it was the hypocrites she had a problem with.

CHAPTER SIX

Women in their forties found a perfect potential partner in Stephen, they found him attractive and sidled up to him at cocktail events every so often but Stephen skirted around them carefully, wary of encouraging them. Those women could be had anytime, there was nothing challenging about snagging a woman in her forties. The challenge was all the *woman's* Stephen was sure. She had to put in the effort, court him, spend money, expend charm and be generally willing to make all the concessions. But that didn't appeal to him. Well before he turned forty he realized the shock value of finding a twenty-something to hang out with. They catapulted him to the forefront at any gathering, the duo gnawing at others' curiosity. Also, these women undeniably showed greater prowess in bed and honed his sexually enterprising nature. His reasoning was unassailable.

His prolific partners had helped him shape his sexual message, giving him an easy confidence and almost no awkwardness when it came to getting a woman into bed. It was amazing how many points guys could score with a woman with suave and assured love making. Consequently, Stephen almost never left home without a packet of condoms. He slipped it into his pocket along with his wallet. A good lay it seemed, was possible at any time, it was really up to him, his knowing pale blue eyes agreed with him when he looked at himself in the mirror as he fastened his tie. With Olivia, Stephen knew his life could take a pivotal turn for the better. Yes, it would help if she could stop tucking into those ribs at lunch. It was incomprehensible to Stephen, how could she? He felt he ought to be able to sue her for jeopardizing such beauty so recklessly. But it was such a Eureka! Or Bingo! Moment that he knew this was it. *She* was it! His ticket out of this constant seeking, questing and not finding AND, he just realized, if she had already been the skinny mini he wanted her to become, he would have had no chance with her, sometimes good luck came in pudgy, ungainly fleshy fullness, he accepted it as his charter to fix that. He would be her catalyst for change as she would be the one to catapult him to that trajectory he'd been eying all along but had never had recourse to entering, until now.

At 57, juggling two or three women at a time, maintaining an active work schedule, he wanted to settle down and maybe have a child? Well, that was a happy thought to contemplate. Olivia would be a perfect accompaniment to the tune in his dreams. Even mathematically she made sense. She had all the parts that were missing in Denise, Emma Joy, Norma and Sandra. She was naturally beautiful, wonderfully soft and she was Martha Bates' daughter. This was *way* better than winning the state lottery, heck, it was better than finding someone to publish his book. 'I mean,' he thought, what were the odds of *that* ever being successful, even if he should beg, bribe or finagle his way into getting published?

Unquestionably, getting Olivia would top every other goal he had aspired to or dreamed of until now. He'd walked by thousands of fiction titles that sat ignored on bookshelves like unsung heroes, Shakespeare's undiscovered minions in the back of the stage, tiny sparks afforded to them through a publication and quickly extinguished, never to be heard from again. The chance element of success in this realm perplexed him no end. How did some things pass for classy writing? On whose word? By what measure? He hated beauty pageants for that same reason, how do you single out beauty from other beauty? He would fail miserably as a judge in a beauty contest he shook his head ruefully, choose one beauty amidst ten beauties, all lined up with the same physical measurements, how crazy was that?

Stephen stared at the blank page on his computer, it was already 10:30, his flight was at 1pm from SFO, his boarding pass was printed out and he had to beat it. He needed to stop in Fenton's office briefly as well. He started to type, *"Olivia, I am so glad you were free to join me for the concert last night. Weren't those surprisingly good seats! I really look forward to seeing you again when I am back in San Francisco on the 14th. Please tell me you will let me take you to dinner, I'll call and confirm."* Pausing briefly, he added,

"You are one of the most unusual women I've met and I already cherish the opportunity of being able to talk to you and hope to soon call you a friend." See you soon! Stephen

His elaborate signature followed his name including his cell phone contact information. He paused, thought for a second and selecting his resume he attached it to the email. He clicked the send button and powered his computer down, packing and moving around all the while. He needed to catch a salad at the airport there was no time to stop for lunch now. He hadn't eaten anything since a toasted bagel with smoked salmon at 6:30 pm the night before, prior to meeting Olivia at the Symphony. He was looking forward to some sleep on the flight. He hadn't slept enough reviewing documents he had to submit early today, paying the price for taking Olivia to the show.

Olivia's day was dogged with email. There were some days like that. She left her office at 7pm that night, struggling out of her chair and hailing a cab upon exiting the building. She didn't look at her blackberry at all, turning on a movie to watch and falling asleep before the first ten minutes were up. She awoke refreshed at 5 am, ahead of her alarm clock set for 6:15 and made herself some coffee, called her mother at 7 after she got dressed and chatted briefly about Markus taking his stuff out of the house. "Give it time my love," her mother was saying on the other side. "You never know, you might change your mind and want him back. What did he do though? Your dad and I loved him so much."

"It's okay mom, let's not go into all that again now. I need to rush off. I went to the Mahler concert last night at the Symphony by the way."

"Did you enjoy that? I always went with your dad, but I guess it's okay to enjoy the symphony alone too."

It was on the tip of Olivia's tongue to tell her mother that she did not go alone but changed her mind. "Gotta go mom, talk to you later, Love," and mouthing a kiss into the phone she hung up looking at some papers and picked up files to take to work. She hadn't done a damn thing last night and she had so much to plow through today.

At around 5pm in the afternoon, she answered the

phone, she had cleared a lot of her backlog and was feeling better, thinking she should get up and get some coffee, "Hello, it's Stephen." She grimaced, how was she going to shake the fellow off?

"Listen, did you get my email?" Email? She thought. She scrolled down looking for an email from Stephen Baylor in her unread messages. She'd been too distracted answering all the emails from the two Vice Presidents she reported to and had completely skipped this one. "No, I'm sorry, I've been busy." She was wondering how he'd gotten her email, had she given him her card? She couldn't recall. Good thing her cell phone number wasn't printed on her card. She usually wrote it down when she wanted to give someone her personal information.

"What are those boogers at Stahlberg doing keeping such an attractive girl locked up?" he demanded teasing her. "Oh come on." She laughed. Her reserve thawed somewhat. He almost never opened his conversation without complimenting her on her looks, it was nice, like drinking an extra cup of mocha, not sure if it was good for you but she was enjoying it anyway. Stephen loved that she laughed. "You know your laugh is so melodious."

"Oh stop now, where are you?" "Why don't you read my email young lady, you will know where I am. I will be back in San Francisco on the 14th, can I take you to dinner?" Fourteenth, fourteenth.. She needed to think for a minute. It was her brother's birthday but since he was in Massachusetts all she could do was wish him over the phone. "It's my brother's birthday on the 14th." She said abstractedly. "Then it calls for a celebration, how old will he be?" Stephen asked. "He turns thirty one." "He's very young to be teaching at Harvard!" Stephen exclaimed. "He's always been a prodigy of sorts." She said. "Is he your older brother?"

"Yes." She paused not wanting to tell him just how much younger she was than her brother.

Stephen sighed. She fit into his criteria, the under thirty club! *Yay!* He thought triumphantly. It baffled his colleagues that at his age, in his mid-fifties, and he clearly looked his age, thanks to his balding head and graying hair surrounding his bald pate which he bore as his crown of thorns, he found younger women to date who were most certainly of enviable caliber. But *none* could come close to Olivia in potential and value. Wait until he'd finished with putting those essential finishing touches to her portrait. Seriously, it wasn't generally hard to pick up girls, especially when they were financially hard up, young, leggy, lovely; Woo them, take them to dinner and to bed, but usually they weren't from the solid stock that he admired so, their pedigree just wasn't there. It felt fabulous touching them and having their soft flesh yield warmly to his caresses but after a few months of it, he felt a distinct feeling of self-loathing, there hadn't been much of a challenge to begin with, for those girls, *he* was the catch, the real value was in finding a girl who was surely *the* catch! Olivia was it! His ticket! He could see it all as clearly as he'd been able to see from the outside of this fabulous party in progress through one of those spectacular windows in a swanky home in the Pacific Heights neighborhood as he climbed San Francisco's many hilly streets one night The opulence and style that bespoke the lifestyles of the very privileged. Olivia would definitely feel at home in one of those. His esteem for her climbed an easy stair.

He administered a rigorous regimen for himself physically managing religious hour-long stints in the gym every other day regardless of how busy his work schedule was. Despite that, he didn't look very young, the biggest drawback being the egg like dome that protruded plainly encircled by a ring of graying hair. Balding had not been a new phenomenon for him. Balding men were often attractive and he knew some men who were balding who felt blessed because women found them to be sexy and smart and more sincere than their hirsute counterparts. It appeared as a greater disadvantage to Stephen because he was so squarely focused on lithe women who had often barely transitioned from girlhood. He was long used to looking older than he was and turned the fact to his advantage with his customers who somehow trusted him for being older and therefore by some default of years, a more responsible lawyer. He did have an impressive repertoire of clients he'd served as well.

He saw Anil walk by his office, so much hair this fellow had Stephen thought. Look at all that hair on his head! Anil had quite the *opposite* problem. Clients often thought he was way too *young*. He always seemed like he needed a haircut. As if on cue, Anil ran his fingers through his hair as he stopped at his secretary's desk to talk to talk to her. At about six feet tall, Anil was just shy of being lanky. He had some breadth of shoulders to decry the thinness and delicacy that is often the bane of many men who strive to attain a balanced look of slimness and tautness emanating from a lifetime in gyms, under controlled conditions. The occasional twitch of his left eye hidden behind thickly framed glasses gave him the nervous look of a geeky college kid in a daunting class. Even so, lucky fellow was what Stephen thought of when he thought of Anil. I mean, this fellow had an appetite, he never seemed to order his food with care and he looked like that and all that hair?? Stephen knew Anil spent hours at his desk, depriving himself of sunlight and exercise? Maybe it was because he was just thirty-four years old.

Wait until these guys saw Olivia, there was a certain removed charm about her that he was finding irresistible and he was certain would capture the imagination of his colleagues as well. It was March now, if he played his cards right, he could be bringing

Olivia to the firm's Christmas party in New York. He needed to hurry. "I need to check and see what my parents are doing, I don't know if Oliver's thinking of coming down." "Wait, who is Oliver?" his voice was almost irate. "My brother, I just told you about him."

"And? He spends his birthdays with his family?" Stephen exclaimed incredulously. "No, it's complicated." She didn't want to have to tell him that Oliver was very attached to their father and he flew down once every couple months and that he had been talking of visiting even if it was for a weekend to spend time with his parents and see Olivia as well. He had said he would potentially try and coincide his visit with his birthday, like he did quite often for their birthdays that way his they could all celebrate that some special event together as family.

CHAPTER SEVEN

Olivia's was a very close-knit family for all intents and purposes although Oliver was never made aware of the family's one skeleton. It was an unspoken bond that none of the others wanted to even try to sever because that meant touching it and touching it would scorch them. Olivia didn't know who was more hurt by the experience, her mother or herself. She never knew if her parents had talked about it. Olivia sometimes recalled those weeks spent with their grandmother when their parents had traveled to Europe and had thought it would be best for the children to spend time with their grandmother instead of bouncing around Europe with them.

Uncle Paul, their father's brother had always visited them when their parents were there. Their father had just one sibling, a sister had been born to their mother prior to the boys but she had died within a year of being born.

Olivia remembered being gathered up in her uncle's arms when he came to visit. He always stroked her and stroked her, straightening her dress out and smoothing it down until she eventually pulled away to share a book she had been reading with him or show him her latest art project. He and his wife had gotten a divorce a few years after their marriage. Uncle Paul said she had taken a fancy to some professor in the college she was doing some graduate work with and that, for all they knew, had been that. All she recalled was her parents being very welcoming of him and ensuring his comfort when he visited.

Olivia was perhaps six years old and had been getting ready to have her Grandma and their eight-year old neighbor Madeleine from down the street, a skinny red haired girl join her for the tea party she was hosting. She was intently organizing her tea things, setting and resetting places when the doorbell rang, Olivia ran to get it. Oliver was out on his bicycle, she could see him from the window and their baby sitter Juanita was taking a nap under the large elm tree out in the back, she was to join Olivia for the tea party as well. Olivia had arranged and rearranged the tiny teacups and had put place names for her guests. She was having trouble spelling Madeleine's name. "Oh Uncle Paul!" She cried in surprise. "Grandma's gone to bring Madeleine to my tea party? Will you be staying too?"

Olivia's plump little arms and face were red with excitement and exertion. Her shoulder length hair blew in wispy curls twirling on her shoulders, her eyes shone bright blue with the fun she was anticipating. Uncle Paul held her soft hand and tugged at it.

"I saw mother busy chatting away with Madeleine's aunt, they are too busy to help you spell anything right now." Olivia's eyes widened. "How do you spell Madeleine, Uncle Paul?" Her finger digging deep into her cheek dimpling it as she contemplated the conundrum of spelling Madeleine.

"Well, I will tell you if you come and sit right here." Uncle Paul's voice was as warm as the weather outside.

He locked the front door and unlocked the door on Olivia's childhood and innocence forever changing her ability to be fully comfortable with men, damaging her confidence in herself.

Olivia didn't know it then but Uncle Paul had caused a blight that froze a part of her that would lie eternally unawakened. Like a blind person never knowing what it was that he or she was missing by not seeing the world because they'd never seen it before, wondering at all the noise seeing people made about what they saw, Olivia also would never know what it would be like to have not had that first sexual encounter when she was barely six.

When Uncle Paul was done with Olivia, she sobbed out loud not sure what had happened to her, hurting with the pain but her overriding concern was that she was not ready for her tea party. "Now look what you've done Uncle Paul!" She cried plaintively. "You spoiled my party. I wore this dress because they matched with the napkins. Now this dress looks dirty." "Don't you spoil your party and say anything to anyone now Olivia, they won't want to eat at an icky girl's party now will they?" He said softly as he smoothed his hair and looked at himself in the mirror above the mantle piece. She ran out of the room and downstairs into her bedroom pulling out all her dresses crying out to Juanita. Uncle Paul was startled to learn the Nanny was so close at hand. He quickly unlocked the front door and let himself out before anyone could see him.

It had been so warm outside that Juanita had dozed off in the shade under the tree, she shook herself awake and came running up. "What is it Via?" She always called Olivia that because Olivia told her she liked it better than Olivia, "That's a long name for a small person like me, O-Livia" she'd said rolling her eyes saying the 'O' when she'd first met Juanita two years ago. She saw Olivia with all the clothes around her. "My dear, you got so dirty setting up your tea party!"

"Let's get you into the shower and all pretty again! It won't do to have you looking like this when Madeleine comes now will it?" Juanita cooed as she undressed Olivia. "What did you do with your underpants silly girl?" She gave Olivia a playful little slap on her bare bottom as she took her into the shower. Olivia choked down her tears worried her tea party would be ruined because she had set the ice cream outside the freezer. She didn't want to think of Uncle Paul's visit.

Juanita was concerned that Olivia was so distraught over the tea party. "I will put the ice cream back in the freezer okay Via? The Ice cream will be fine." She tried to calm her down and dried her tears as she combed Olivia's hair and twirling it until it bounced back into bright blonde curls. "See how beautiful your curls look, just like the princess in the book!" Olivia smiled shyly and hid her face in Juanita's skirt. "Can I go into the freezer too and come back okay?" Olivia asked Juanita. Juanita laughed and tickled Olivia, "You are a funny little girl Via."

Olivia looked on at her anxiously wanting to become complete again, regain firmness like the ice cream but not knowing how to go about it.

Later that night their mother called, "How are you darling?" Her voice made her seem so near and Olivia gripped the phone hard. Her brother had finished talking and had turned on the television and Grandma and Juanita were talking about plans for tomorrow. Olivia's voice caught a sob when she heard her mother's voice.

"Mom, where are you?" Her voice came out in a soft, plaintive tone. "I have to tell you something." "What is it darling?" her mother asked, "Grandma was telling me about the lovely tea party you had for everyone and how nice the tea was!" Her mother said cheerfully.

"No, I want to tell you something else. Something about Uncle Paul." Her mother didn't seem very interested in hearing about Uncle Paul. It was close to midnight in New York, they had just arrived after traveling all day from Paris. "You can tell me later my love. We will be home tomorrow. Do you want to go to the burger place for dinner tomorrow night? We'll have them fix you that Mango Ice Cream Shake you love so much. Why don't you tell Grandma we will all go out to dinner tomorrow."

When her parents arrived the next day Olivia held her mother more tightly than ever. Her mother noticed her daughter looking wan and asked her mother-in-law,

"It has been very hot here this summer hasn't it?" She blew at her daughter's curls gently to clear the

71

moisture. "Well, we don't get more than two or three of these days before it starts to cool down again here." Her mother in law answered.

After their burger dinner that night, her mother promised to go up to her daughter's room to read to her. Oliver was allowed to watch television and Martha carried her daughter to her room.

"So how was your tea party yesterday?" Martha asked her daughter, setting her down in bed. "Brush your teeth and come and I will brush that lovely hair of yours while you read me a story." Olivia brushed her teeth, all the while turning around to see if her mother was still there, waving to her. When she returned, her mother had selected a book for her to read. "Would you like to read me this one?"

"I read a lot when you were gone mom." Her mother smiled. She was exhausted and needed to slide into bed but wanted to hold her daughter for a bit. She hadn't seen the children in ten days. This was the longest she'd gone without being with them. Olivia snuggled into bed, "Why do you look so tired sweetheart?"

She sensed Olivia's difficulty in breathing like the catch and miss of breaths between sobs. She tickled Olivia's stomach, "I'm the one who's been on a plane!" Olivia chuckled and held her mother's hand. "Mom, Uncle Paul was here yesterday."

"Really? How come Grandma didn't tell me?" "Grandma was not home, she had gone to fetch Madeleine for the tea party."

"Did he bring you any presents?" "No but mom, you know what?" "What?" Her mother ruffled her daughter's hair and stifled a yawn. "Uncle Paul dug me hard here with his finger, it hurt." "What?!" Martha's sleep flew out like a frightened bird. "Where Olivia?!" Her voice took on an insistent tone. Olivia was surprised at the sharpness in her mother's voice. "Here." She pointed to her panty. "He did *what*? Oh my God! My baby!" Martha was aghast. "Where was Juanita? Oliver?" "Juanita was outside and Oliver was on his bike. They were coming to my tea party." Olivia didn't know what to make of her mother's expression. Martha spent a few more minutes with her daughter and when she saw Olivia's eyes drooping in sleep, she staggered out of the room. She caught a hold of Kevin's sleeve and tugged at it as he sat watching the television. Oliver sat next to him and Kevin's mother was seated on the sofa across. She couldn't see her daughter-in-law pull at her son's shirt.

He reached over and patted his wife's hand, "Come sit for a bit or are you very tired?" He turned slightly to see his wife. He straightened when he saw her expression. He mouthed, "What's wrong?" She gestured to their bedroom upstairs and walked away wearily.

"'Night Mother, I am exhausted, I'm off. Good night son." He ruffled his son's head and followed his wife upstairs. He was very sleepy also.

His wife closed the bedroom door behind her and turned on the television to drown out the conversation they were soon going to have. "That bastard Paul, *that bastard Paul*." "Paul?" Kevin was flabbergasted, "What did *he* do?"

"He raped my daughter, our daughter, our Olivia." Her eyes had a dry wetness to them her voice sounded ragged with the effort she made not to raise it. "Are you out of your mind? *Paul rape Olivia*? What next?" "Kevin, it's true. Listen to me, I just talked with Olivia." Her disheveled hair and distraught face stopped Kevin from questioning further.

Kevin's eyes had turned a deep, intense brown. He looked gravely at his wife. "Can I talk to Olivia about this?" "No you will not. Plus she's sleeping now." "How? When?"

"I don't know, but she told me that Uncle Paul stuck a finger inside her and it hurt really hard. She thinks it was a finger Kevin, well I don't know if it was a finger or more than that." She sobbed into her hands. Kevin swallowed. He felt a rush of bile rise in his throat.

"He was here yesterday apparently but no one else saw him." "What if it was someone else and not Paul? It can't be him. I mean, I'd know by now if he was a shitbag like that." He rubbed his hands on his shirt they had become clammy and wet. This was alien to him he felt like a being from outer space.

What kind of questions do you ask following something like this? His face looked drained, his clenched jaw holding back further expression. "Did you check her to see if she's hurt?" "She was in bed when she started to tell me about it. I didn't want to have her relive that experience, there was no way I was going to subject her to an examination."

"But you have to!" he said in helpless fury. "I will, when I bathe her tomorrow." Martha didn't want to rekindle her daughter's trauma in anyway. Sleep eluded both of them. Martha woke up early and had almost drunk a whole pot of coffee as she waited for her daughter to wake up. At 7:30 Olivia woke up and after playing with her and beating Oliver at a game of Scrabble that morning, she urged the children to the pool outside. She helped Olivia undress and noticed a very slight redness but she was unable to tell any more. Even as she fought her revulsion she resolved to take her daughter to the doctor for an examination all the while thinking of the ramifications that would involve.

The doctors would insist on knowing more and on investigating the issue to the extent necessary.

When they were in the pool the next morning, Kevin came out of the house white faced and stood looking at the scene. The yellow and blue candy striped ball bounced around like an insult on the water of her tragedy Martha Bates thought, as the kids ducked and dodged throws. Martha scrambled out of the pool at the sight of her husband's pallid face and wrapping a robe around her dripping body she went inside. Kevin said that he had gotten a call from the coroner's office.

Paul's car had driven off a hill and had rolled down in flames killing him, he was purportedly alone. There was no immediate report as to how that could have happened. The views on Highway I could not only be scintillating and distracting but also, as it proved in Paul's case, deadly. No one would ever know if Paul's death was deliberate or an accident caused by the sheer beauty of a bewitching California coastline. The lot of them were speechless, what happened in the hours and days afterward did not include a visit to the doctor as Olivia's parents had planned.

In a daze that typically follows sudden tragic events resulting in the termination of peoples' lives it was a matter of coming to grips with a new reality. Martha was never able to reconcile with Kevin after this incident, however unfair it seemed that he should have to pay any price. She felt irrevocably violated often choking back sobs, convinced that her daughter's innocence from that day forward was posthumous. She was also certain there was nothing Kevin could do or say that could offer reparation. Kevin on the other hand felt cheated out of an explanation by Paul's death. He spent time with his mother in the weeks following his brother's death dealing with the police, insurance companies, Paul's employer and his mother's suddenly aged look. She desperately clung on to Kevin, her eyes wildly chasing answers to the many whys that made dizzying rounds in her head following Paul's death.

Some facts that emerged troubled Kevin. He couldn't share them with his mother as she was wallowing in the throes of grief and he didn't see any point in revealing a facet of Paul that would set her emotions in a further tailspin. When he got home later that night however he shared them with Martha. She had returned from a new book tour and was completely drained out. He noticed she looked tired and had lost weight in the week since he'd seen her.

Juanita was with them full time now caring for the children, driving them to school, tennis and swim lessons. Oliver played the violin in school and was a bit of a prodigy they were learning to their delight.

The children were asleep when Kevin thought it was not a bad idea to broach the subject about these reports he had uncovered about his brother's past. He had never known for instance that Paul had had a restraining order issued by one of Paul's ex-wife's friends for indecently handling a child in their home. Neither his former sister-in-law nor Paul for that matter had ever raised the issue.

Kevin was shattered by this information. How could he have known so little of his brother? How often did the fellow hold Olivia in his arms? The thoughts spinning in his head like captured flies in a jar were too tortuous to handle alone. He wanted to draw Martha into his ring of sorrow. She was the fair one, the one who could see through bizarre characters, make them up and also make amends for them. As a writer, it was her gift, her prerogative and her duty. Martha had absented herself from the tragedy of Paul's untimely death he thought bitterly.

At the crux of it all, he had lost his brother, the thought of what he might have done with Olivia made it seem like Paul had died twice in the same night in Kevin's mind. These two realities were too jarring for him to contemplate in one sweeping thought. It seemed like they both deserved a separate consideration. He wanted to talk about this dichotomy of his feelings with Martha.

That night however, Martha was unprepared for Kevin to bare his soul to her. While she was reading from her recently released book in a store earlier that day she had had a rare moment of losing control and had blanked out. She couldn't read the words on the page in front of her. Her thoughts went back to Paul's act with Olivia, getting his fix. Martha apologized, the gathered audience clapped anyway and after mumbling through the rest of the time in the giant bookstore with the store manager doing a valiant job at maneuvering the questioning she made her escape with her assistant.

She cut into Kevin's recounting of his brother's suspected past. "And you are telling me you had no clue about this fellow's problems Kevin? You and your mother live in constant denial. For heavens' sake, its guys like you that were bystanders at the holocaust." He had always loved his writer-wife's use of hyperbole, it made conversations that much more titillating, evoking laughter and proving her point but Kevin didn't know he was deserving of this harshness. He remained silent as she picked up her pillow and left the room, signaling the first of many nights when they would not share a room. The incident had wedged itself between them building a wall neither one had the energy to climb over.

If Paul hadn't died, it was possible both Kevin and his wife would have done something to take him to task, to vent their anger to seek justification in whatever measure possible, but with his death, they felt that opportunity snuffed out. Kevin was too overwhelmed and felt engulfed in a cloud of ambiguity by all the implications of what had happened and chose never to bring up the subject again. He became more introverted with Martha and was the parent who was more physically present with his children.

Kevin's work as an architect was local. It was amazing how much Martha had to travel to itineraries set by her publishers. Several of her books had been optioned by filmmakers, some enjoying tremendous successes at the box office, others more moderate. Her overwhelming readership was unanimous that the movies sucked and they could never hold a candle to her books.

CHAPTER EIGHT

Martha rarely joined them at family get-togethers. Often it was just Oliver, Olivia, Kevin and Grandma. Nowadays Olivia made that long slow drive from San Francisco to Carmel each time, taking Oliver with her from the airport to have a meal with Grandma if her dad was too busy to pick him up. They tried to car pool but it didn't always work. Her dad was an architect and lived in Palo Alto, close to where he worked. Her mother had her home in Carmel but traveled to New Mexico with her new partner often these past two years it seemed. She did explain she had bought a home in Albuquerque.

"So what's your answer Pretty One?" Stephen queried Olivia from the other end. "Can I let you know in a couple days please?" Olivia said buying time. She scrutinized her email, scrolling up and down, not finding anything from him. "Hmmm, I don't see it?"

she said puzzled, certain if he said he sent her an email, he would be right. "Wait, you don't have my email address do you? How did you manage to send me an email?"

"I worked with a guy at Stahlberg a while back and know the email convention you guys use." His voice was smooth. "What do you think it is?" She queried. Firstname.lastname@stahlberg.com, he sounded pretty triumphant. "And the last name you used was...?"

"Well, Olivia Bates right?" "Not right."

"I beg your pardon" His voice dropped a notch. He wondered at the task at hand now, how was he to pass off Olivia Unimpressive last name as Olivia Bates? He grimaced at the unnecessary hurdle this new fact had opened up in his nicely laid out plans. It would have been one thing to introduce her as Olivia Bates.

"I have my father's last name, Bates is my mom's maiden name." "Well, I didn't get a bounce back somehow." He was a little upended but was careful not to be too vocal with his concern about her last name. "What *is* your last name?" His point blank question made her pause for a few moments. "Stephen, what exactly are you after?" Olivia had never basked in the glory of her mother's renown. "Excuse me. All I'm doing is trying to send you an email, not a letter bomb!" His voice was indignant. He had used this strategy before. A careful blend of outraged morality tinged with a hyperbolic metaphor usually did the trick, caused them to back off at the tone of righteous indignation, worked even with topnotch lawyers. He didn't think Olivia had it in her to trump moves he practiced on the average New York lawyer.

"I don't know." She laughed to diffuse the tension. Not fully convinced she wanted to give him her correct email address but knew that he could potentially find out what his father's last name was, her parents' divorce was all over the Internet. Large chunks of talk show programs had been devoted to their split up.

"That's just it, that's why I sent you an email to show you I am for real, I have a real job, I work my butt off and all I am asking is to take you out to dinner. I find you extremely interesting and attractive, I'd like to get to know you better."

"My dad's last name is Campbell." Her voice came in softly cutting into his harangue.

"Oh, Scottish I see." Stephen didn't want to continue in his belligerent vein lest he lose her altogether. He immediately typed her new email and forwarded the old email to her new address. She received it instantly and opened his email curiously. She gasped at the fact that he attached his resume, '*What a moron!*' She thought at first glancing through the contents and closing the email. She sent her brother an email instead, asking him what his plans were for his birthday and if it would be in order for her to throw him a party and could he make it on time?

Oliver responded almost immediately from his blackberry telling her he wasn't sure if was going to travel back to the "Left Coast" as he put it, he had purchased a bicycle in a store named 'Left Coast Cyclery' in Berkeley some years back with his father and had been struck by the name since then. Brother and sister used it routinely to describe California, but if she was going to throw him a party, maybe it wasn't such a bad idea after all, adding a wink at the end of his note.

She wondered what she was getting into with Stephen. She also wondered what she would say to Stephen now should Oliver tell her he was going to be able to come. "I was thinking it would be easy for mom and dad to come visit at my place, they don't seem to have issues that way and you are welcome to the spare bedroom in the apartment as always, now that Markus is not here..." She ended inserting a grimace into the email.

Stephen had also gotten engrossed with an email from Ruby. He cleared his throat, "Sorry sweetie, I didn't hear what you said." She pursed her lips at the 'sweetie' and said, "That's because I didn't say anything."

"Did you get my email?" Stephen's voice was anxious.

His familiarity with technology wasn't as fluid as his familiarity with Intellectual Property law it would seem. "I did." She refused to acknowledge his resume in fact she resolved not to.

"I will have to see what my family's plans are and get back to you, it depends on whether they want to do something private or if Oliver can handle a party. I'll have to play it by ear." The resignation in her voice rang a warning bell to him. He immediately responded, "Oh don't you worry, have that time with your family." He swallowed. *What he wouldn't have given to actually meet and shake hands with Martha Bates*! He could only imagine how *validating* it would be to casually drop this at a dinner after a tough day's work with the guys. *'Like I was telling Martha Bates, her characters would fit in just as well in Denver or Miami.'* And watch their eyes leave their sockets.

Of course, he wasn't going to tell Olivia that, it was his private thought, as private as all those attempts he had made with hair re-growth techniques that he'd never shared with *anyone*. *His baldness was his personal crown of thorns, that* private, he thought.

But this, this *opportunity*, this *god send*, whatever you wanted to term it, to work on the delightful challenge of converting Olivia, well and rounded to Olivia, to becoming a gorgeously chiseled beauty was too enticing, the reward too palpable just in and of itself.

To think of the ultimate other plusses. Oh god! Her family?!!!! No, do not screw up Stephen, he thought and vowed that he would tread very carefully. She was no New York lawyer and he wasn't going to subject her to any of that aggressive style anymore.

"I'll call you tomorrow."

"Sounds good," she said and hung up. She waved Robert in when she saw him outside her door.

Stephen started to see the image emerging from the shadows to claim its place in the screen. All he assigned to himself was the humble role of the framer. The mirage he saw with Olivia didn't have to be a wispy mirage that evaporated with the onset of reality, it was his picture, he needed to put the right frame around it, sometimes the frame was more expensive and needed more deliberation than the art work, he knew that. This was a rare original that he would hang on his mantle, the palette with all the right mix of colors was poised in front of him waiting for his unique stamp.

CHAPTER NINE

When Stephen saw Olivia next it was a rainy San Francisco night with windswept streets that were largely slick and fast emptying as early as 7:30 in the night. He picked her up outside her office building in his cab.

Seated inside the restaurant, he looked at her carefully after the waiter had taken their coats. The moisture in the air had turned the tendrils surrounding her face into an alluring frame, her eyes looked larger and he wondered if she'd shaved off some weight maybe? A few, mostly unnoticeable pounds if you moved past her face and saw the blouse folding twice over the waist.

He wondered at that. That was going to be his job but

he knew he wouldn't dare venture on that path until after he'd had some luck getting her into bed. *That was key*. Never start on any mission to alter a woman until you've had her under you. Literally under you, that was his rock solid belief. You can salivate on possibilities as soon as you spot the right woman but don't start to be didactic preemptively. Once that threshold was crossed, the equation often shifted. Just like all those thousands of letters from credit card companies soliciting your clientele and the minute they managed to convert you as a client, they had you where they wanted you. *Then, and only then,* the fine print came into effect. He didn't think of himself as a predatory credit card company but the analogy seemed only too apt as he pursued his current goal.

Who knew? Olivia could well be a trump card who could potentially mean he could work on ridding himself of the layers that Denise, Norma and Emma Joy formed around his personal life. It wasn't his fault that all these women came in such limited packages. There was no denying he needed a woman, well, er, fairly often. It was the nature of his work he told himself, plus whom could he blame for his surplus testosterone? All that dry legal stuff, those reams of pages of banality needed an offset. The legal profession existed because people could not be trusted to behave with fairness and needed referees in the playground of life. It was too taxing. The demands placed on him were enormous. Although he'd not been an exemplary lawyer, his had been a solid resume that did the rounds on proposals to high profile clients. Being with a woman recharged him. He employed newer, more imaginative techniques to charm the women into succumbing. His shrewd eyes watching their resolve break down, like ice sculptures melting in the wee hours of the morning at the end of a party, where their initial aloofness, seated in seclusion made them seem unreachable. Yet they were all susceptible to the vagaries of the warmth in the air, of the neglect of their creators and the boredom of their audience, they did melt into nondescript water. Everything evolved.

Sometimes Stephen wondered how his colleagues managed spouses and their professions and didn't suck at one or the other of their commitments. He juggled his various interests simply because he refused to let them develop into *relationships*. The word relationship had a cumbersome connotation to it. He liked to think of them as arrangements of convenience, not unlike marriages of convenience that European royalty in the past frequently indulged in to keep their financial and political fortunes intact. Now, he had all these experiences meld into one big whole that sat in front of him in the form of Olivia. No one else he could think of had come this close to fitting the bill. It would be a challenge to get her where he wanted her to be, a size 0? Don't push so hard he told himself. Maybe he would settle for a size 2, but he wasn't one to give up because the going got tough, that stuff just spurred him on even more.

Olivia was smarting from a difficult family gathering. Her parents had been on the verge of a terrible argument in front of her Grandma, Oliver and her. Olivia had ordered in Indian food for Oliver's birthday. She'd kept the *naans* warm in the oven. The dinner was delicious by everyone's account, even normally hesitant Grandma ventured on the chicken curry and *naan*. Oliver had brought a couple bottles of good red wine. Her mother had had a melt down because Grandma had suggested that Olivia shouldn't have been burdened with serving up dinner after a long day's work and that Martha could easily have organized something.

"After all it's your son's birthday." She sounded more self-righteous and protective than she'd intended perhaps. Kevin, glad to be with his children and his former wife, who he still loved, spoke without thinking and laughed out loud saying, "If Martha could serve up her books, she'd feed us, but food, no."

Martha clearly didn't find that funny. She left soon after dinner, forcing them all to abort their dinner and digress to dessert and had Oliver cut the cake Grandma had baked. When she left her face was hot and her eyes looked moist.

Martha was a statuesque woman. Olivia had inherited

her coloring and her hair but had taken after her paternal grandmother in her roundness. Oliver was exactly like Martha, tall, lanky, artistic, he often was able to calm his mother down much more effectively than anyone else. "Come on Mom, that was just a joke." He whispered into her ear as he helped her into her coat.

"It may well have been my love, but I have to go. I promised to grab a drink with a friend anyway." She bent down to kiss Olivia, waved goodbye and was gone before their father could say anything. Kevin shook his head in disbelief at this sudden exit and turned his attention back to the food.

"Did you get this from the same *Maharani Restaurant* we always loved?" "Yes." Olivia was relieved she could talk about the food. "Here have some more." She held out the bowl of *chicken tikka masala.* She was often mystified at the suddenness of the tension that built up between her mom and dad. They both seemed such awfully reasonable people, fair, thoughtful and sensitive and then boom! There was mom going off the handle.

She hadn't slept very well the following night and had not eaten all day that day, her face looked wan and there was an air of fragility about her that excited Stephen. "So how was your dinner with your parents?" "Fine thanks." She swallowed. "Did you just fly in?"

She noticed the carry on bag he had stacked against the wall next to their table.

"Yes." He sighed.

He ordered a bottle of wine with dinner and she drank a glass, he finished the rest and they left, both distracted with their separate problems. When he insisted on taking a cab to see her home she looked at him, "Where are you staying?"

"Well, I have a room always available at the Hyatt." "But that's in the opposite direction." She said. "I can see myself to my house in another cab." It had stopped raining now but more rain seemed imminent. He debated quickly what the best thing to do would be. It was after 9pm and he had had a long day. She didn't look that excited about further company either. "Listen. I apologize. I've been a poor host. Can we meet again tomorrow night for dinner?"

"I can't." Olivia responded, "I can't let you keep taking me out to dinner every other night, it just doesn't feel right." "Well, you can cook me a dinner perhaps?" his watery blue eyes looked tired but earnest and beseeching under the streetlights reflecting in the shining wet streets. "I am no great shakes in the kitchen." She muttered, not sure what to say. She ate out often. On days she was going to be home she brought home packaged salads from grocery stores and popped into the microwave a pre-made pasta to go with it, opening wine on some nights and beer on warmer nights. She used to hang out with her girlfriends on Wednesday for a drink as they had dubbed Wednesday the mid-week sucker and insisted on cheering themselves up somehow. All of that had changed after she and Markus started dating and their eventual engagement. Things had been different living with Markus, he had liked to throw things on the grill some nights and it had served her fine. She let him do the cooking and she stacked the dishes in the washer after dinner. It was amazing how being with a guy on a regular basis, getting engaged and following that up with marriage was such a transition of habits, trading one ritual for another.

"Tell you what. I'll grab a pizza on my way and bring a bottle of really good wine. You set the table and make coffee at the end of the meal." The rain had started to come down softly again.

Olivia wondered often about this night. It was a turning point night for her. She could have said no and walked away but she didn't. The waiting set of cabs that the doorman at the restaurant had called for them, the fact that she was tired and needed to end the day, the fact that Stephen looked so heartfelt in that uneven night light with the swooshing sound of tires as the cars made their way on the wet pavement nearby, egging on the urgency. "Sounds good." She shrugged acquiescing. She could always change her mind in the morning she thought.

"I'll email you tomorrow to get your address." He held her cab door open for her as she slid in, leaning forward to brush her hair with a kiss. He hurried on with his bag to the other waiting cab and she gave the driver her address.

When Stephen's email came later in the morning asking her for her address, Olivia had had such a trying morning with one of the Vice Presidents that she felt she needed to vent in front of someone completely removed from her work environment.

Stephen was a lawyer wasn't he? He would be able to parse this out for her. All those Ivy League degrees shining on his resume could be of some use perhaps. Her face took on a sardonic look. She typed in her address without much ado and hit the send button without stopping.

When Stephen arrived at her home Olivia was far more composed. She looked chirpy even. This was the first time he was seeing her in less formal clothes. It was pizza night then. She wore a long sleeved maroon colored thermal T-shirt over a pair of jeans and looked even younger with her hair pulled back in a high ponytail.

He walked in holding a pizza above him, sausage with fennel, sun-dried tomatoes and whole olives. She could smell the olive oil. It smelled delicious. She took the wine from his hand as he set the pizza down on the counter and turned to survey her apartment.

"My, my" he muttered, "So this is where the Beauty lives and sleeps." He looked around admiringly. Her dark brown leather sofa set was embellished by a beautiful large wooden chair with a dramatic orange and brown paisley pattern that caught the light from the lampshade next to it. The still life painting above the fireplace with a pear in shades of green and an apple taking on orange and pink hues gave the room a dramatic effect. The side table had a smattering of photographs on it with a clutter of unopened bills, letters and magazines all shoved together hurriedly. Stephen didn't want to ask too many questions about the pictures, noting that she was with a young man in more than a few of them, the young man could be her brother or her recently estranged fiancé. He wasn't going to let anyone else become the focus of the evening. She hastened to say, "Well, dad got me that chair several birthdays ago and my brother got me this painting a couple Christmases ago. He got it at an art sale in Boston." She had set the table for two with a small tea light candle lit at the center. She had deliberately removed the taller candleholders her grandmother had given her. That would make it look too romantic and intimate. This way, the casualness of the evening would not be threatened.

The pizza from *Nioni's* was freshly made and perfect. She got out ice cream after dinner but when he emphatically refused to have any, she put the carton back in the freezer without helping herself to any.

He wondered how he could get this beauty to be more conscious of her food intake, ice cream after pizza for grown ups at this hour? *Heresy!* He looked down at his blackberry. "Shit!" he exclaimed. "Can I go online here?" He inquired as he tugged at his computer from his bag. She nodded, not quite knowing what to say. He sat on the sofa and she told him how to get online. She went into the kitchen to put the dinner things away and sat down across from him with a book to read, letting him work quietly. She wondered when he would leave.

He seemed fairly engrossed with his email, opening files and documents on his laptop. "Would it be awfully rude of me to ask for some coffee?" he asked.

She noted how tired he looked. She got up and made coffee using her Bodum French Press. "Black, no sugar please." He glanced up at her as she brought it to him. "I'm sorry Beautiful, is it okay if I send these emails off? The gang is working on finishing these off and submitting first thing Monday so I guess they will be working through the weekend, they are up at this hour in New York, it's after one in the morning there!" He exclaimed, hoping to impress the urgency of the situation upon her.

"That's fine. I have to finish reading this book for my book club anyway." Her book club met on Monday nights. She sank into the sofa, tucked her feet up and started to read, setting the cushions comfortably around her. She soon drifted off to sleep. She awoke to find Stephen looking down on her. She sat up with a start. "Gosh. I fell asleep." Her cheek was warm and pink. He said, "shh, I didn't want to wake you. I finally finished sending that email out." She stood up and brushed against him. He held her hand. "Olivia, I couldn't stop thinking of you in New York." He said softly as she looked away.

"Stephen, I.." She hesitated and he held her chin and turned her to face him. "Don't say anything please, just let me kiss you." He bent down and kissed her warm face and yielding lips with assured mastery. Olivia was surprised at herself responding. Markus had been a couple of years younger than her. She had never dated anyone more than two years older than her. This throbbing excitement felt odd. Her face flushed as she looked away. Her hair had come undone from her ponytail or she couldn't remember if she'd removed the clip while reading.

Stephen curled her hair around his finger, "One strand can cover my head fully. What do you think little girl?" She laughed to rescue herself from the embarrassment.

"I guess you'll need more than a strand. It's not all that bad really." She said touching the top of his head. This line always worked for Stephen. There was an innate maternal streak in most women, they wanted to protect the trampled upon. If women were more like men, wars would be an endless, ongoing reality. Thank god they weren't.

Women were the reason there were fewer wars in the world, Stephen was convinced of that and he wasn't going to stop and consider Helen of Troy, those were Greeks.

Olivia tried to find her slippers and stumbled back into the sofa, Stephen sat down beside her and continued to kiss her again. Murmuring and kissing, he moved her into her bedroom. Their clothes came apart, shoes got kicked off in what felt like a practiced rhythm. Stephen lifted her breast to his lips like he was taking a closer look at a rare flower and was soon encompassing her entire breast into his mouth working his tongue on her nipple until she felt the looseness in her limbs disassembling her reserves. He deftly put on a condom as she murmured weak protestations, he felt the heaviness of her waist and buttocks on his hands and he gave her a firm caress and squeeze, noting how urgent the task at hand was in slimming her down, no, scratch that, that was too mild, *thinning* her down.

They made love again two hours later, his excitement at the prospect of *Project Olivia* driving his desire to new heights. Olivia had never been with anyone who had been so free with her, what was the right word? So *not* tentative. Stephen seemed to know exactly how to arouse her, awaken a primal instinct for pure physical intimacy that she'd never explored before, had never felt invited to explore before. Stephen knew his moves exactly, knowing just how to get her body to respond. What was it he had heard or perhaps read? Ten thousand hours of anything would make you perfect at it? Well, he'd put in his hours for sure.

It hadn't been as difficult as with Emma Joy. That girl had been a tough son of a gun. Olivia was more giving? Pliant? Could he say that? Emma Joy was certain of her sexual prowess, very sure she was bestowing huge favors on Stephen. She was more than aware of her worth. Sex with Emma Joy was a test for Stephen. He felt like he'd passed the New York Bar Exam afresh each time he ended a night with Emma Joy without breaking up. Their lovemaking was tempestuous and usually followed a pouting, almost breaking-up fight. Stephen matched her temper with an equally fiery one of his own to show her he was not cowed down by her youth or incredible appeal.

Olivia's refinement was supple. She seemed like she didn't wanted to etch out a distinctive character for herself at the same time it felt like she didn't want to be like someone else? Stephen couldn't tell if it was her mother she didn't want to be like? Sometimes celebrity children suffered, abashedly carrying the burden of their parents' halos reluctantly trudging forward, looking cautiously to step out of their ominous, awe inspiring shadows.

Stephen had studied so many women so closely over the years he knew they modeled themselves often after their mothers following childhood experiences and other situations that formed the mass of most life experiences. Emma Joy had had a cruel stepfather - Stephen had guessed something of the sort early on in his relationship with her. He felt these women gave it back to men they became intimate with. They were often genial, loving creatures at the outset but there was a cauldron of frustration that bubbled very near the surface and erupted unabashedly before or after lovemaking. That was why he knew that any kind of permanent relationship with Emma Joy was out of question, getting her to agree to one would have been nearly impossible of course. If Emma Joy had to settle for Stephen, it would be for something much larger than fancy degrees and expensive dinners, it would have to be because he had a private plane or something. It happened every day, Emma Joy knew that. Stephen was merely a stopgap measure, an able tutor as she headed on her way to the man who *did* own a plane. That part of their arrangement was fairly unambiguous.

The arousal Olivia felt with Stephen was unprecedented and furthermore unmet in the future. Years later, when Olivia watched her children working the monkey bars in her backyard, her brown skinned son's dark, long lashed eyes looking at her triumphantly as he swung with one arm...She often recalled the feeling of being transported by Stephen into a world of pure sexual pleasure that she'd never experienced with anyone before or since. No one could work her breasts like Stephen and awaken and animate the recesses of her physical self, touch parts of her that she'd never knew existed. No, not even the love of her life now, her husband.

CHAPTER TEN

When Stephen returned to his hotel the following morning. He stopped at the concierge and ordered flowers to be delivered to Olivia. He paused to hand him a hand written note that he put in an envelope to accompany the flowers. Olivia had gone on a long walk after Stephen had left in the morning. She had made him another cup of coffee and he had seen himself out. She wasn't going to stand at the door waving to him.

When she returned from her walk she realized she had left her cell phone in the apartment. The doorman handed her the flowers. She knew they were from Stephen although she'd never received flowers from anyone until now except from her parents and Grandma a few times in college. Markus had not been into that type of thing and Sean, Greg and two other

guys she'd known had all been too young to bother
with flowers and such niceties. Markus had picked a
bunch from the flower patch in the apartment complex
to give her for Valentine's as they headed out to dinner
the previous year. That had been it with regards to men
and flowers up until now.

She opened Stephen's accompanying letter:

*Olivia, Last night was unbelievable on so many levels.
Being with you revealed things about myself that I
never knew about. I cannot fully describe the intimacy
of that feeling. I need to see you more, to see myself
fully. Trite as it may sound, you fulfill me.*

Unabashedly YOUR,

Stephen

She read the letter again and carried the vase up to her
room. She first tried to set the flowers next to the sofa
that Stephen had sat on but moved them to the kitchen
counter because they filled the room. It was an
extravagant bunch of premium long stemmed roses
ranging in colors from ice pink to dark fuchsia
managing beautifully to echo the message in his note.

Stephen left for New York immediately upon
showering. He went straight to work and was sucked
into the details of a pharmaceutical client that was
looking to extend the initial patent on. With deadlines

looming, he worked in a round the clock frenzy. Anil left around 8 am on Sunday morning stating he hadn't showered in more than twenty-four hours. Stephen couldn't help but admire Anil's impeccable intuition and reserves of energy, both mental and physical. Between the two of them they had the entire package ready to be filed on Monday morning. Stephen traveled to Connecticut to meet with his client on Wednesday and it wasn't until that night when he was headed back to his hotel in a cab from the station that he realized he hadn't called Olivia at all since that eventful night.

He groped for her business card which he'd saved with his credit cards so as not to lose it with the mess of other business cards he carried in a separate card holder. It was almost six O'clock in San Francisco. He wasn't sure if she'd be in the office, he didn't have a cell phone number for her yet. Olivia answered the phone on the very first ring. "I'm coming right down." She said into the phone without looking at the monitor. She thought it was the security person telling her that her cab was here. She gasped when she heard Stephen's voice on the other end. "Olivia, are you there." "Hello?" Her voice was inquiring. Where had he disappeared to? How dare he take off like that without a word? What was he thinking? He could just screw her and leave?

She had been enveloped with a terrible sense of self-loathing these past few days that she could barely get herself to eat or sleep. She had deliberately stayed until late at work each day so she didn't have to replay the scene from Friday night again at home. She swore she would never be such an utter fool again.

All those thoughts broke lose in her head like children escaping their classrooms at recess as soon as she heard Stephen's voice. She heard her own voice come out in a stifled sob. "Olivia, darling, oh don't cry baby, don't." She clung on to the phone and cried soundlessly. "I must be the worst kind of slut you have ever met." She managed at last.

"*What?!*" His voice was shocked. "That's nonsense. Listen, don't cry. I am crazy about you. I will come over on Friday night and spend Saturday with you and take the red eye back on Sunday. I cannot risk letting you feel that way." He felt awful for having neglected to so much as call or email her. The poor girl, no wonder she was so distraught. He was exhausted but he had to go back and see her. He could not jeopardize losing her, he was just getting started, of course he was a sloppy screw-up for having forgotten to write to her or call her these past four days but he had been under the gun, he'd even missed going to the gym.

She hung up. He got off the cab, went to his hotel room and sent her an email.

"Olivia, please understand, I had to leave for an

emergency soon after I left you on Saturday. I went straight to my office and didn't go home until Monday. I apologize a thousand times for my thoughtlessness. Please forgive me."

She read the email a few times and saw he was trying to reason with her. She wondered if he would follow through on his plan to visit the weekend. He arrived on Saturday morning and took a cab to her apartment without calling. He called her from the lobby below. "It's me, Stephen, can I come up?" the doorman looked at him not sure what to make of him. Was this fellow Olivia's father's friend? He wondered, *'What do I care? Fellow's as old as me, he can't be going out with Olivia now can he?'*

She asked him to come up. He found a marked difference in her. She looked a lot more vulnerable and, was he seeing right? Smaller? He took her in his arms and kissed her. She stopped crying after some time. "I just thought this was it, here was this guy who comes to my house, sleeps with me and forgets all about me." She flicked her fingers, "Just like that."

"Don't insult yourself so." He said, shushing her. After they'd made love, he took her out to lunch at the famous Greens Restaurant ordering with care.

Her initiation into the *Baylor Method* had begun he thought as he squeezed her hand across the table. She looked around self-consciously to see if they were being watched. "Let me order for you since I am quite familiar with this place." He ordered the French Lentil Salad and the Papardelle. "We'll share the food." He seemed to know his way around here. The waitress who took their order explained the caloric virtues of their selections.

"Fabulous choices, you can definitely treat yourselves to dessert." Stephen waved her away. "We'll see about that," trying hard to steer clear of the word dessert. After lunch, they walked all the way to the edge of Fort Mason. It was getting cold and they huddled together hurrying back to their car. Her body was alive and responsive to him. She wanted to experience Friday night again. When they returned to her apartment she took him to the elevator straight away with a quick nod to the doorman. She didn't owe him any explanations she was sure of that, certain that his disapproving gaze followed her into the elevator. The doorman had looked away. Of the sixty four units in the building, there were far too many possible variations and permutations to how people chose to live their lives. His job was to ensure front desk operations ran smoothly and no miscreants slipped in on his watch. He shrugged at the veiled snub from a normally kind and chatty Olivia.

When they emerged from the bedroom Olivia was convinced this had been the best possible experience she'd had with a man. It was unlike any other. She wouldn't know it but it was because no other man she'd been with had had a similar breadth of experience with women. Stephen had mastered the art of pleasing a woman so well that he had a sexual adroitness in bed that impressed, excited and aroused Olivia as it did other women, leaving her and them yearning for more.

Later that night, they went out for a walk, he raced her uphill and waited for her to catch up. She marveled at his nimbleness, despite being so much older than her and suddenly wanted to be as agile and swift as he was. She winced at the difficulty she was having climbing uphill when Stephen had pretty much sprinted up with apparent ease.

"Tell you what Gorgeous," he said pulling her forward and kissing her as she at the top of the hill after her panting subsided. "If you did this thrice a week, you would outrun me any day." He was careful not to mention that she should also halve her food intake and that it would also likely transform how she looked. "Oh well." She laughed and clung to him as she regained her breath. She gingerly made her way back as he held her hand, steadying her on the way down. They crossed two young women on their way up who were making a quick climb up. Stephen kept talking to Olivia but was so distracted by the youth and beauty of the women coming uphill that he would have rolled down if it hadn't been for Olivia's hand to steady him and keep him from falling. He turned to look at Olivia, the contrast seemed so stark that he did not apologize for almost rolling down the hill with her due to his negligence.

He was too overcome by the image of a narrower Olivia doing this jog again uphill with him in that very same jogging suit one of the girls was wearing. It was possible, quite the touchable mirage. "It's like how smaller cars are easier to maneuver and use less gas? We become food guzzlers and then feel as flexible as Hummers.." She nodded, "You mean inflexible.. I get it." he nodded. "I guess less is more kind of thing huh?" He nodded again fighting to keep the satisfied gleam creeping into his eyes.

She was struck by the image of Stephen diminishing under the weight of his diminishing self. Was he programmed or what! But soon they reached her apartment and as a reflex she opened a box of cookies and asked him if he'd like tea. He left the cookies untouched and watched as she picked and nibbled on one. Before she could reach for the next cookie he closed the lid and sat back, drawing her close to him. "I can't believe I have to leave all this loveliness and return to New York." His hands were running up and down her back.

"Are you trying to stop me from eating another cookie?" She turned squarely on him. "Why? No." he was caught off guard and was bereft of a response. He hadn't expected such a direct question from her. He should have known, she was not obtuse, only somewhat reticent at certain times. Something that just didn't add up in Olivia, in all of Stephen's careful calculations with how most women he knew worked and what made them tick.

He had a surprising propensity and facility in courting women and could figure fairly accurately as to what made them tick. There could have been factors about Stephen that were attractive to these women; maybe it was the aura of wanderlust in him, a romance of his image that he had so carefully cultivated, maybe they wanted to be the thing that nailed him down to permanence.

One of the reasons women responded to him with some eagerness was because of the likelihood that each felt confident she would be successful in securing and tethering him, in being the one to enable his final docking. Some were thrilled by the challenge of fighting a potential foe they saw in the lure that New York City held for Stephen, like it was a woman. They felt pitted against the city, for the magnetic grip it had on Stephen, these women felt the ecstasy of vying against a metropolis, although they could never articulate quite that sentiment to curious members of family and others who were stunned at their daughter or sister or friend's obsession with Stephen, the academic, serious looking lawyer who talked way too much, whose teenage crush on Shakespeare had matured into full blossomed love as he grew older. A love he foisted on his women as methodically and with the zeal of a missionary looking to convert to the fold.

Stephen sensed a lurking insecurity in Olivia. A Bug. Something that sat deep inside her that was responsible for her responding to his calculated advances, like she was intrinsically programmed to respond to them. He knew it was not just his marvelous sense of timing or judgment, or, he was quite proud of it, his prowess in bed in satisfying her, it was more than that - it was Olivia. She had some deep- rooted need to yield to him.

That thought nagged at Stephen. Was she as 'manageable' by anyone? What was her give? Why was she not more resistant? He pushed the thought away trying to enjoy some of the ease of his success.

The adrenaline rush of a chase wasn't exactly present in this case although the fact that she was Martha Bates' daughter was a high in and of itself. He wasn't going to get off of that high in a hurry.

In the months since he'd come to know her, he had steadily become her de facto personal trainer. He was the guy she raced up the hill and now surpassed in speed, the woman who picked a salad with alacrity in restaurants, the woman who seemed to have less time to eat the cookies sitting on her fridge so much so that she had stopped buying them. Ever since Stephen had walked back with her from work one evening, when he had gladly carried his heavy computer bag and accompanying files to her apartment, he had insisted they didn't need a cab, she had been startled at the possibility of doing that, of walking back from work, all the way uphill to her apartment. Yes, of course she had a gym membership, who didn't in the city? Why for heaven's sake, her parents' had the membership at the old place in Carmel still going, that's what her Grandma told her. Olivia went to the gym as often as she could, she averaged one trip a week and rewarded herself with a dollop of cool sherbet to welcome herself back to the world of 'unsweat' she called it, or that's what Markus and she laughed about when she returned from her gym and he had finished playing a new tune he was practicing on his guitar. She wasn't all couch potato for sure.

Olivia had never, before that day, contemplated walking back to her apartment. She had either walked the few blocks to the train or had sat in a cab when she was in a hurry. It had never occurred to her that the distance was walkable. That *that* should come as a revelation to her, a city girl, more than surprised her, it chastised her in a way. It perhaps came down to cab fare and the availability of it and not having to think hard or weigh her options for saving a few dollars. She realized that despite how sleep starved and exhausted he was, Stephen had done it that day to instill the thought in her, to show her it was possible to walk back from work to her home. She struggled in her high heels that day and he talked of how women in New York and perhaps in San Francisco as well, carried a spare pair of shoes they pulled out from their ample purses to put on once they got to work. She considered his comment and tried out his idea in the weeks following.

Stephen had to show these New York colleagues of his who were so stoked by the thought of celebrity, that he was sleeping with one. One who was so eminently desirable physically and otherwise. Among the many theories that spun around in Stephen's head was the one that seemed to bear testimony to his keen observations of couples. His perusal yielded results as follows: Average to good looking men who married fabulous looking women ended up doing average in their lives. What with this arm candy they sported everywhere they went, they didn't need any more validation that they'd scored. *Those* men married to plainer looking women, on the other hand, aggressively climbed social, career and success paths with acute diligence. They *had* to prove they weren't second fiddle to the guy sporting that exquisite blonde on his arm because *they* on the other hand, had the luxury of a vacation home in St.Tropez, fancy cars and boats and the works which somehow compensated for marrying 'unequal' to the men who had clearly appear to have stolen the punch line with their choice of woman.

When Stephen expounded on this theory one night with Ryan and Anil over dinner one night in New York, Anil remarked, "Hey Stephen, is that your way of keeping us off of the pretty girls so we pursue success rather than be pleased with holding a beautiful woman?" Ryan threw back his head in laughter, "Not a bad strategy Stephen!" Stephen's comments had been prompted after seeing a couple seated across from them in the restaurant that had led to his expounding on marital gratification and the crucial parts good looks or the lack thereof made in the rounding off of success factors.

Stephen wondered at getting together now following Olivia's dazzling transformation. What would that do to his theory? Oh well, every once in a while there were exceptions to the rule. There were many power couples who were devoted to each other and both husband and wife appeared to be prize catches, but those surely were the exceptions, his assumptions were talking of the norm, the general body of men. He was exceptional, there was no reason why his union with Olivia couldn't side step that norm and be part of the exclusive club. He was warming up to the idea real fast.

He paused for so long lost in his thoughts that she

wondered if he'd heard her. She let the subject drop. He probably was trying to stop her from getting that second cookie. Her mom had made faint references to her daughter's propensity for all things dessert but she'd been so subtle that it was a light touch and mostly go; never insisting that she try an apple instead of the apple pie.

He cautioned himself and looked at a note pad lying on the corner table and avoided her question completely. "Do you write as well, Beautiful?" he asked her. She was getting accustomed to these endearments. He rarely called her by her name, just appropriate endearments that capped off each question. It was something he'd learned very early on in his lengthy chain of relationships over the years, confusing names of women in bed showed such awful lack of class. That's why dating outstanding looking women made it that much easier as the endearments rolled out more naturally.

"Well, not anything like my mother's writing of course." She said and put the book inside the drawer not intending to share any more. He was curious. The beauty had other distractions besides being some kind of marketing manager for a financial firm. She also dabbled in writing. He knew she had some friends, her closest friend Allie had just moved in with a boyfriend of over two years and therefore was less available than she used to be. Olivia herself had been out and about with Markus these past three years that she'd become sequestered from what might have been a routine with her other girlfriends and weekend meet-ups.

Stephen had 'happened' upon her during that hiatus. He couldn't help but marvel at the value of timing. It had certainly been a stroke of luck. The road ahead with Olivia seemed about the best possible of roads he'd seen in many years. If managed properly, it would be like he had arranged the numbers of the pinball machine that spat out the state lottery numbers, anointing a winner. He would succeed in Gaming the System.

Only once, in his more idealistic years, he'd fallen completely in love with a Philosophy major at Columbia who had been his classmate. She had been an enchanting girl. Her father's family had been investors in the railways all those many decades ago. She had been everyone's unreachable star, a vision who spouted poetry and expounded philosophical viewpoints on meal options in the cafeteria and had several young men attendant to her whimsy. Her advocacy for vegetarianism had been so persuasive that even Stephen, the proud carnivore swore off meat when they dined together.

Stephen's life up until then had been monotonous, his parents lacked adventure or creativity, his mother, bless her heart served up predictable dinners at a set hour each night. Stephen's mother had originally been from Idaho and had met his father as a young girl on a trip with her family to visit an uncle in Denver. His father's family members were long time Denverites. Baylor Senior's brother and sister used to live within a fifteen mile radius from their parents until the parents died and their sister moved to New Hampshire to live with her daughter who had twin sons with health issues, leaving her brothers behind in Denver.

Stephen's mother had raised him on a staple of potato and meat dinners. His palate had opened up enormously after his move to New York. He had honed it with fastidious care, assiduously learning and reading about French, Italian and Spanish foods and wines, learning early on it was as important as learning to play golf to get ahead in business as to demonstrate that assured *savoir faire* about international foods. Plus, he was dealing with clients who routinely traveled the world and in that regard Stephen was a homebody. His work had kept him so chained to the three locations he served as an attorney that he hadn't seen very much of other states., let alone other countries. He often longed to visit Alaska and Hawaii, that would be tantamount to an international trip for him but he never took the requisite two weeks off that would be imperative to do justice to visit these places. It was how he managed to stay with some of the more interesting and controversial accounts the firm had in the industry vertical he served.

"I used to want to write when I was younger, in fact I have a half finished novel somewhere." He rubbed his eyes wearily. "Really!" Olivia was excited to learn that he too wrote. "What kind of novel? Espionage?"

"Well, if you really want to know, it is historical fiction, set in Renaissance England." He yawned. "Can I see it?" "Maybe, if I can get a hold of it." He said dismissively. "I will leave now and when I come in the morning, we'll do that run up the hill again. Won't we Gorgeous?" He tried to soften his voice so he didn't sound like a grade school teacher. She heaved a sigh.

Stephen realized he couldn't get peeved at Olivia for any reason. She had been more malleable to his machinations than he had anticipated and clearly there was undeniable value in pulling this through to the finish line. He could only see the benefits multiplying as he got closer to her. Olivia's mother could potentially oversee his book getting launched. Didn't she have the power to wave her magic wand with the publishers? Everything was a function of habit in his opinion. Martha Bates had habituated herself to producing this endless string of successes. He was in the habit of selecting the prettiest girl on a train or a party and investing the time to craft the worthier ones to a stage he considered perfect enough to showcase like works of art above a fireplace or a mantle piece. One could will oneself to do anything *but* grow hair on one's bald patch, he was completely convinced of that.

Losing weight was such a small challenge relatively. He knew, he'd fought off all those potato pounds diligently from his college years in Connecticut and later. It was the only way to get a pretty girl into bed in his opinion. Of course back then he didn't have to contend with lack of hair, he had had a full head of hair then. This balding business had started only in his thirties and had been swift and aggressive. "Okay, what time?" Olivia asked. They agreed to meet at 8 am before he left.

Sadhana Seelam

CHAPTER ELEVEN

Olivia climbed down the hill slowly. She was doing Stephen's climb routine. *La Methode Baylor*, as she had come to dub the habit she'd cultivated, the regimen she'd inadvertently signed herself up for was growing on her. It had been about three months since she'd first met Stephen. She hadn't realized she had to do so little to lose so much weight. It had never occurred to her to shed calories because she never considered herself overweight in the first place, nor did anyone she'd known commented on it.

Her biggest incentive to climbing that hill was the relish with which Stephen ran his hands over her body, his fingers contouring her lines, spanning her waist, circling it, murmuring, exclaiming, telling her she had "less than half a span to go" before he could span the back of her waist with his hands. It may have been an exaggeration but she thrilled at the suggestion at the prospect of holding his interest, at the idea that his eyes would stop seeking out every other young woman who walked the streets of San Francisco. She disciplined herself to eat dinner by 6 pm each night, so she gave herself enough separation from her last meal before sleeping each night. She could repeat this in her sleep now, of course, Stephen always said this as if it was something he practiced himself. It appeared like he was telling her the guidelines he imposed on himself and she couldn't take offense at him for that. *Chew slowly, enjoy every calorie you consume, value it. Almost never take the elevator, unless you have to climb over seven floors.*

Really? She had thought then, he is surely nuts!? Her office was on the 16th floor, so that wasn't an option. BUT, she realized. She could climb a few and then take the elevator. The first few days, she climbed up to the third floor and then exited the stairwell to take the elevator.

On the following Monday, emboldened by her now routine climbs up the hill across from where she lived that Stephen had started her on, she climbed to the seventh floor and then took the elevator up. It felt like there was less of her to lug up the stairs.

It was so liberating, this ease from the bulk of extra

weight, like she was suddenly climbing without having to carry a suitcase up. She recalled what Stephen had said to her, it's the same logic as fuel-efficient cars, they are fuel efficient because they are lighter, "you need a lot of gas to lug around a Hummer, Beautiful. Or hadn't you noticed? Those little smart things that run up and down in a mighty hurry, those are so nimble, they should mandate that no one can drive a car bigger than a small four door sedan from say 8 am until 5 pm, wouldn't that be just the ticket to getting us out of this oil mess?"

He laughed as he spoke, twirling her hair around his fingers, playing with her earlobes, "Less is more even with food." He wove his pearls of weight loss wisdom, intertwining them with other issues, somehow making it all that much more of a relevant and acceptable garland of commonsense.

It was almost ten weeks now that she'd started doing lunch like she was in grade school again. She'd packed a sandwich about three times each week for lunch. After a breakfast of yogurt and granola or a biscotti and coffee or anything that normally took her fancy for breakfast, her breakfasts had never been very heavy duty affairs; BUT she *had* to have coffee every morning. It served the same purpose as her alarm clock, woke her up, she didn't stop adding milk or sugar, she liked her coffee that way and nothing was going to stop her, not even Stephen's "Coffee should be all black or else it can be called something else but please don't call it coffee," would convince her to drink coffee his way. His eyes had popped out of his head when he saw how much sugar she spooned into her cup of coffee. He edged his cup away in mock fear lest the habit became contagious. She was obstinate in her resolve to never give up the one thing she liked waking up to, rich, creamy coffee with a generous helping of sugar. Stephen knew better than to try and persuade her away from it, it was important when people were trying to lose weight to stick with some cravings, it harnessed the reward element and helped them stay truer to a new diet.

Her colleague Robert found her to be full of sandwich excuses at lunch. "Oh I got a sandwich today," had become a steady refrain. "You walk home from work, rarely take the train back with me. What's wrong with you?" He inquired playfully. He knew she'd broken her engagement off with Markus and was careful not to probe too much. She was taking this very badly, the poor girl. He liked working with Olivia. She was so straightforward she could be one of the guys, like any one of his soccer friends he met twice a week at practice. His fiancée had loved talking to Olivia at the departmental picnic a few weeks ago. "She's so refreshing!" Coming from his fiancée who was non-committal about most people, it only served to underscore how he felt about Olivia. Robert couldn't help noticing how skinny (!) was that right? How skinny Olivia had suddenly become. Really! Where was that amble that was hard to ignore as Olivia walked from her office to the printer or from her office to the elevator just a few months before?

Olivia's transformation hadn't occurred overnight. It had been painfully gradual, she had finally gotten around to checking her weight at her gym two weeks after she had started on *La Methode Baylor*.

Olivia almost never went to the gym these days but had gone to the gym to check her weight because she never kept a scale in her house. Markus had often shaken his head in disbelief at this bizarre tendency of Olivia's not to own a scale. "Scales don't bite you know?" He'd joked but was irritated because she wouldn't hear of him buying one and he wanted to have a scale around to check the weight of his music instruments and luggage as he flew frequently to Los Angeles teaming up with friends to play at some events.

She weighed one hundred and forty eight pounds! Had she really knocked off close to ten pounds in less than two weeks? She couldn't believe her eyes. The last time she had checked her weight was in her doctor's office when she'd gone for her physical, she had been almost a hundred and sixty pounds then, her doctor had suggested that she get more exercise and had made some menu suggestions and offered to refer her to a nutritionist but her overall caveat had been, "Your weight is only an issue if it impedes you from doing the things you want to do, you are active as far as I can tell, you will be quite fine in due course if you managed your diet and introduce some rigor into your exercise routine." Was it because she'd known this doctor for the duration of her stay in San Francisco that they had both gotten used to each other and didn't notice that she was, Olivia paused, *'overweight?'* Or was it because the doctor herself wasn't that healthfully apportioned? Olivia couldn't bring herself to be uncharitable to her doctor however.

Doctors can only do so much and how pray do they tell a happy patient who appears completely comfortable with how she looked, attested to feeling healthy and leading a fairly active life, that she needed to fix something? Most people stopped short, Olivia thought they didn't feel the need to fix something that wasn't broken. She had thought similarly, until now. Now suddenly, she ached for the feel of Stephen's arms around her, his cooing embrace telling her how much he loved her body. He'd praised her to the high heavens but of course had yet to compliment her figure, because, she looked at herself defiantly in the mirror, waging a warring argument, there was nothing redeeming about her body. She upbraided herself so vigorously that she went on a rampage tossing things into the trash can from her pantry shelves and her refrigerator, gone were the ice cream buckets, the tins of cookies, the jars of shortbread munchies her Grandma had gotten her from her trip to England. She felt weak after the exercise. She went to the trash chute and tipped her bag down that she had tied in seven spirited knots afraid they'd climb back up and reclaim their positions on her shelf and in her refrigerator.

Olivia's friend Susie who had bailed on their lunch plan all those many weeks ago on account of being straddled with a sick son asked her if she wanted to join her at the gym that night. Olivia turned her down "I don't go to the gym all that much anymore." "Why not Via?" Susie's voice was surprised but tinged with concern, "Don't tell me you are moping away for Markus. Listen, I saw him at Eric's the other night, he's hurting too, you two should try and talk things over." Olivia quickly withdrew from that conversation.

Olivia was getting adept at brushing friends and family off when the broached the subject of her broken engagement. It was amazing how, after breaking up with Markus and with Stephen's entering her life, she had made herself so scarce that people naturally deduced she was hurting from her break up with Markus. *'Little do they know that I am so over Markus and all that.'* She felt guilty at the facility with which she had transitioned her affections from Markus to Stephen.

It was very likely that she didn't get to fully capture

the loss of Markus because of the confusing presence of Stephen in her life. Going out with a guy almost her dad's age, who seemed to be on a mission to transform her into some sort of *showpiece?* Was that it? She was reluctant to unravel what this meant. For the moment she was reveling in the learned advances of a man who seemed to shower her with affection even with the attentions of some stunning looking women who were purportedly his lovers not so long ago. She wanted Stephen to allow her to join their ranks. These were imagined demoiselles who were impeccable, without sin, awe-inspiring and all of them grateful for Stephen in their lives.

Olivia turned down Susie's invitation to go to the gym, pulled on her running shoes and ran down the five flights of stairs and sprinted some two plus miles to the stairs at the Coit Tower and sprinted back again. She was doing this three times a week now. She returned home breathless, she had forgotten to take her water bottle with her and had grown dizzy during some parts of her run but had made her way back an hour later, peeling off her clothes and stepping under a scalding shower hoping the super hot water would burn some sense into her. Wrapped in her robe with her hair tied high above her head in a drying towel, she let the tears flow. What was she doing all this for? For this part-time lover? Why hadn't it ever occurred to *her* to want to not be so overweight? Why did it take Stephen's little *Baylor Ballad* as he laughingly called it singing to a tune that straddled Rhapsody in Blue and Take Five:

Kick the fat slack Hit the thin sack Calories out there galore Lose your daily count Before you take any more

This silly little ditty albeit set to a great beat he had conjured up was an incredible accompaniment to her daily running routine, up those impossible climbs, down steep and sometimes slippery ways, her ears thrumming with music ranging from sounds of Carmina Burana renditions to Stephen's ditty that he'd sung to her that she'd managed to transport to her iPod.

What resonated most was his methodical insistence that weight was a numbers game that stacked up with the aging process, "If you think about it Beautiful," his fingers running over her body warm from their love making, "on average adults gain 2-4 pounds a year on a conservative estimate from the time they stop growing vertically and continue to expand horizontally." She had laughed at that. "And you would know of course Stephen, right down to the last ounce, how people gained weight and what not." She'd played a little drum beat with her fingers on his head making him chuckle, "Just so Beauty. Just so." She stopped being sarcastic with him after a while because of how smoothly he seemed to take in his stride her skepticism and the tremulous trust she started to place in him like a candle sitting near a window, holding on to its flame from being extinguished, the winds of disbelief had blown strongly from time to time but she was getting adept at drawing the blinds on time and soon, keeping them down, keeping the flame alive.

Would she have never broken up with Shawn her boyfriend from years ago had she been slimmer? It had never dawned on her that despite her fairly involved relationships with some of the guys their eventual rejection of her had been because she had been deemed *'fat?'* Should she be even more grateful now to Stephen because he had rescued her from that syndrome? Would Markus have made a bigger push to be more amenable to her likes and desires had she been slimmer? Did people treat her more lightly because she was heavy? How would it be if she went out with Markus now? On a whim Olivia picked up the phone and dialed Markus's number. She wanted to ask him to join her for dinner at the café two blocks from her house where they'd often gone to get dinners when they were together. Markus didn't answer his phone. She hung up without leaving a message. Hours later when she got Markus's text telling her he hadn't heard his phone ring as he was with some friends, she replied, *'oh, I was calling to ask if you mistakenly had taken a book I was looking for, but I found it, take care.'*

She hated that she had lied to Markus. Nice, honest Markus with his mop of curly black hair and ever present grin. What was she thinking? She went to her bedroom and took off her robe, her eyes widened in surprise at how shapely her body looked. She had gone lingerie shopping two weeks ago and these sure looked good on her. She recalled the time Stephen was walking back to her apartment with her after dinner one time, "Fatness is a habit Gorgeous, that's what it is, just like cracking your knuckles or jerky hand movements, so," he said as he guided her on the crowded Market Street in San Francisco, skirting pan handlers and a teenage kid rolling on a skate board, pants clutched in one hand, progressing precariously amidst all the obstacles, "staying thin soon becomes habit forming, soon half the slice of cake will be more than you can handle, soon, a slice of cake will be overkill." She looked wonderingly at herself now, half a slice of cake, so true, she didn't eat any of those cookies nor did she crave them any longer.

A week later she was on the phone with Stephen, "It's raining and most uninviting outside, I can't go running today." She moaned. Stephen was wrapping up an email to a client. He spent time with his emails, sitting diligently at a computer calibrating his responses never resorting to a pat reply from his Blackberry. He managed his communication with scrupulous diligence. He moved his computer away to concentrate on Olivia. "Hmm, cold and wet eh?"

He was searching for something to say to her that would serve not only to reassure her but also inspire her. "What you could do Sweetness is walk on the balls of your heels, in your apartment, in your pajamas, you can do it barefoot if you like." "On the balls of my feet? Wait how?" Olivia queried trying to stand on the balls of her feet and falling over promptly. She steadied herself and laughed into the phone, it's not that easy. "Yes it is. Steady yourself and keep walking, do it for twenty minutes for starters, turn on the TV, do it watching Jeopardy or something." He glanced at the time, yes it was just shy of 10 pm his time, which was close to 7 pm California time and she could do it now if she got off the phone and let him get on with his email.

He got an excited email from her later that night, "You know, that wasn't so easy but it certainly wasn't impossible, my legs feel so much tighter after that routine. I was watching Jeopardy throughout *and* I got the Final Jeopardy answer right and the three players didn't!"

"My girl, what can I say?" Stephen sent her a quick note early in the morning before heading out to the gym.

Stephen came down two weeks later to find a slimmer Olivia hidden inside the larger one's clothes. "Aren't you going to buy new clothes to celebrate your new look?!" He exclaimed. "I will, I don't think I'm done yet though, do you?" He didn't know how to answer that one. "Of course Angel if you wish to drive yourself over the edge with this weight loss thing, it will have to be your idea, don't blame me!" He edged away dramatically shielding himself with a magazine from a supposed assault from Olivia. She laughed at him, "You are the devil!" Later that night as they sat on the sofa watching TV she asked him how he'd thought up the walking on the balls of your feet idea, "Oh, I tried it myself when we were locked in with a week's bad weather and power outages everywhere, including the gym. Seemed to be a great way to exercise my legs." "It can get monotonous though so I started to do one length of the living room on the balls of my heels and the other on tip toes! It was very difficult to keep track and the variety kept me going for more than an hour before I realized it!"

"My my! The beauty doth have her own creative instincts, you are doubling up on me young lady?" He said raising her chin to give her a kiss. Stephen saw his onerous schedule looming in front of him that Thursday and realized he would have no chance to be in San Francisco for almost four weeks. His calendar was increasingly getting swallowed up by those blasted East Coast appointments.

Olivia's less demanding work schedule left her with more time. She spent a few evenings indulging herself shopping in downtown San Francisco buying sweaters, slacks, shoes and skirts to go with her new look. She was amazed how she now looked at items of clothing she would never have considered her type until not so long ago. She stood before her wardrobe, taking off clothes from hangers that she couldn't imagine wearing anymore, comfort clothes that had encased her plentiful pounds in woolly, expandable stretch. She paused to look at a picture on her bedside table with her parents and Oliver some years back, she looked *fat* in that group of people. Why hadn't it ever occurred to any of them to tell her to back off of eating so much or pushed her to using the gym more?

When she returned to her apartment laden with new clothes and trying them on going back and forth from her mirror to her wardrobe, she paused to look at herself in her lace underwear, she didn't feel any triumph at her new look. Her thoughts were roiling around in the churn of a pre-tide sea. She was straddling guilt and triumph and didn't meet her eyes in the mirror not wanting to wallow in either.

She lay back in her bed staring at the ceiling, surrounded by all her recent purchases, feeling empty. She imagined Markus walking in on her and seeing her new form, how would he react? She didn't care to know she thought. Her feelings did a dance running up and down the field like players in a baseball game, the ball alternating between being Stephen and Markus.

She felt a deep hollowness like her new lightness had excavated her feelings and buried them under a heavy stone. Her tears rolled down uncontrollably. She felt she'd paid an awful price. She was losing all sense of feeling. She reached for her phone and sent Susie a text to cancel dinner plans. 'Can't leave work tonight, something came up.' White lies came to her rescue like ever present lifeguards at a summer beach. She was getting so adept at giving excuses she felt that in the shaping of the new Olivia. Her spontaneity had been squeezed out of her.

Stephen had visited once again three weeks later and had noticed her looking *'fragile'* dare he say? He was immediately distracted by an email he received from Anil. He left without spending too much time with her although he had made reservations for them to see a play at the Conservatory that night. He was profusely apologetic but was loathe to hand her the tickets lest she invited someone else to go with her. *'Who knew?'* he thought, looking at her, his pulse quickened at how exquisite her face looked with the candle light casting shadows on her cheeks and her eyelashes, lengthening them across the bridge of her nose. When she had entered the restaurant that night, she was noticed, Stephen was always tuned into the entry his girls made. Wearing a shirt tied loosely at the waist with a thin leather belt and a pair of flattering skinny jeans and Mary Jane shoes, Olivia was only aware that she was almost twenty minutes late and not of the entry she was making, Stephen on the other hand couldn't help congratulating himself silently that *La Methode Baylor* was indeed working.

She found Stephen seated at the table with a drink. He kissed her, marveling at the attention she was getting and sat across from her. He certainly didn't want to give her the tickets. Who was this fellow Robert she mentioned frequently at work. What if she took him to see the play? He told her he got a rain check for a future play at the Conservatory. She blinked. They did that? The Conservatory refunded unused tickets? She wondered at that but didn't say anything.

Stephen bid her a regretful goodbye that night. His arm slid around her waist far more readily now when he held her outside to give her a hug, she sized up nicely to his measure. A couple walking into the restaurant turned to look at them and the girl whispered rather aloud to her boyfriend, "Gosh! Talk about being with a rich uncle!" Stephen murmured something into Olivia's ear to distract her, he overheard the comment as he was closer to the door, he hoped Olivia hadn't. Although he was used to a lot of that over the years, especially when he was out with Emma Joy, who flaunted her looks and her young body and dressed with some effect of a hangover from her teenage years. He couldn't risk Olivia seeing anything odd about their union. The comment however, gave him a thrill.

Olivia's roundedness had tapered so effortlessly it seemed, like a line drawing in an animation film. God, he'd give anything to continue to hold her right now, to dwell on the difference he'd help etch. He had to leave for Denver because his mother was having eye surgery in the morning and he had promised her he'd be there. He would be flying out the same night to New York if all went well.

Olivia assured him her weight loss wasn't all that effortless, "It was a massive about turn on the foods in my pantry and my endless exercising Stephen!" She wrote to him once. 'At the core of it all, it's so elemental. Calories in and calories out. I have gotten it down to a very natural reaction that my body has the obligation to abide by. Pitt the amount I consume versus what I burn off." Reading her email, Stephen felt he deserved to do a victory lap around his Manhattan hotel room. How do peacocks do it? Unfurl all those feathers? He would unfurl his if he had them.

CHAPTER TWELVE

Olivia's mother invited her to a party a friend of hers was throwing at his Monterey mansion. Sensitive to her daughter's recent break up, Martha Bates had asked Olivia to bring a friend along. The party was on Friday night and she told her daughter that she needn't worry about driving back in the night because she herself was going to the party alone and had reserved a suite at the Hyatt Regency. Olivia mentioned this to Stephen and he was infuriated he couldn't be there. Olivia was glad. She wasn't ready to introduce anyone to her mother at this time, least of all some funky lawyer from New York in his mid-fifties, however fancy his credentials were or the law firm he was with.

Martha Bates looked fabulous in a dark blue skirt and an orange and blue patterned silk blouse. She wore colors with such grace Olivia thought. Olivia chose an olive colored chiffon dress with silver high heels and let her hair loose opting to wear a large quartzite bracelet on one hand. Her mother came across the room to give her a hug. "Honey!!" She exclaimed. "You look practically starved!" but she couldn't stop herself from following it up with, "You look beautiful love!" She exclaimed drawing Olivia toward her friends to show her daughter off, "All, this is Olivia my daughter." Olivia nodded shyly and accepted a glass of wine that someone offered her on a tray. She found Rachel her one time neighbor from Carmel sitting and texting away busily on her phone. Rachel looked up and found Olivia in front of her, she shrieked and jumped up to give Olivia a hug, "You look marvelous! What have you been up to in San Francisco? How's Marky boy doing? Getting ready for the wedding?" Rachel gave her an appraising look, taking in the 'less is more Olivia' as Olivia glanced away. Her break up with Markus had been so recent that not many of her friends had heard about it.

She shook her head. "Oh no!" Rachel plunged her face in her hands, "I am so sorry!! I should have looked around to see if he was with you before opening my big mouth." Olivia put her hand on Rachel's, "No, it's not bad really. I am the one who broke it off."

"I am so sorry." She said giving Olivia a quick squeeze, "I'm sure you have your reasons, want to talk about it?" Olivia shook her head. "But," Olivia reached for Rachel's hand again and pulled her away to a corner, "I'm sort of seeing someone else."

"What? Already?! You look so stunning no wonder the guys are gunning for you!" "Oh! Stop." Olivia said as she drew Rachel aside to talk. "I know!" Olivia grimaced. "This was a completely bizarre thing and I don't know it's got any teeth to it."

"Who is it? Is that why you broke up with Markus?" "Not at all. It was all over with Markus before I even met this guy." Rachel knew Olivia too well she wasn't one to two-time anyone. She was just too straight for that. "I told you this because my mom is going to try and hook me up with guys she thinks are eligible at this party."

"Don't worry, that's not likely, the youngest guy here is a good twenty years older than we are!" Rachel laughed heartily. Olivia stiffened. She and Rachel had been in high school together, Rachel had gone off to study in Europe after high school and they had kept in touch because they liked each other but also because they had a circle of friends from the smaller community of the Pebble Beach campus of their high school. Now with Rachel's little offhand comment, she wondered if it was wise to tell her about Stephen but she decided to wait. Rachel had started a high end boutique in downtown Carmel that sold some European labeled clothing for women and interesting accessories for men, "That way the men come in and don't get bored when they are shopping with their wives." She had said once.

Olivia noticed Rachel's cream silk dress that landed just above the knee cut beautifully with a cowl neck and opal earrings. "I love this color!" Olivia exclaimed, changing the subject about men. Clothes and fashion was always a safe bet plus she could learn a thing or two from Rachel. "It's the first time I don't see you in black."

"I've abandoned black." Rachel said dramatically, then looking at the shocked look on Olivia's face she said, "well, not entirely, you know. I wear black but mix it up. If it's a black dress, I drape a colorful shawl or if it's a pair of black pants, I almost always wear a brighter blouse. Black needs offsets, we are getting old girl! We both turn twenty eight this year!" She vigorously shook Olivia's hand. "Twenty eight is not a terrible age to be Rachel, stop it!" They went off to get another drink together.

Olivia's mother had made it to the party expressly to see her daughter. She wanted to find out how Olivia was coping after breaking up with Markus. She talked with her children often but it was far better to get a good look at them from time to time.

Back in the hotel when Olivia emerged from the bathroom in her pajamas, her mother gasped, "Darling!" Olivia looked down startled wondering if she forgot some item of clothing. "You've lost so much weight, *what is going on?!*"

"Gosh mother, you gave me such a scare!" She sat on the bed. "Do you like how I look though?"

"I've always loved how you looked my Princess." Her mother leaned forward to kiss Olivia squarely on her forehead. "But you look positively *thin*! Are you sure you are okay?" Martha was convinced Olivia was not taking her break up with Markus well.

Olivia didn't divulge anything. "Oh, I've started to walk from work." "But that's insane! It's more than a few miles and a lot of it uphill, after a day's work. Why are you slave driving yourself like this? Are you short of money?" Martha's voice was incredulous, her pitch reflecting her concern. Olivia shook her head vigorously.

"No!" Her mother wasn't happy. She circled her fingers around Olivia's newly thinned wrist.

She didn't tell her mother what she was really doing. Stephen had given her a few streets that she should consider scaling, of course he had used his special touch to take the edge off of what could appear laborious, "Let the people on *these* streets see this San Francisco Beauty!" he'd exclaimed as he put together a path for her to run, starting from Ghirardelli Square at the cable car turnaround and follow it all the way up Hyde turn around and walk back down or pick up the walk on Telegraph Hill.

"Stop it Mom!" Olivia snapped, nervous that she would spill the beans on Stephen, she knew she couldn't bring Stephen up as a potential partner with her mother, her mother would never ever be able to take it. She saw her mother's shocked expression at her unnecessarily forceful statement and she said more gently, stroking her mother's arm, "Mom, you have no idea how wonderful it is to be a size 2. It feels so right. On days I am tired, I take a cab, stop making such a deal about it."

Olivia started her own questioning, the best way to stop her mother from keeping on about her. "Why did you say you were angry with Abby your editor the last time we spoke?"

"Oh honey, please don't mention that to anyone! I was just going through you, know, a phase. I'll turn fifty eight next year dear, I guess my menopausal problems are visiting me a tad late!" "I was reading *Plum Wine* the other day mom, who edited that?"

"Why that is ancient! It was Abby." Her mother exclaimed. "I liked it so much. I liked how the woman's obsession with her father's mistress long after her mother's death ends only after she meets her in a restaurant. When the mistress had no idea who she was talking to. How did you think that one up mom? That was such an unlikely story."

Her mother breathed deeply and spoke drawing from her trough of memories, "It came to me when I was in a waiting room in a hospital. I was very young then and I'd gone to see how my dad was doing after his knee surgery. I overheard an argument that a father and daughter were having about his dying wife. He had a mistress or lover that predated his wife's illness but the daughter was distraught that their father had abandoned her mother at such a time. I thought it could be interesting as a story. Writers often need only a kernel and then their minds conjure everything else up." Olivia nodded.

"Yup, I guess. That was your third book." "I know." Her mother's voice turned reflective, "I've had about forty since." She was more interested in hearing of her daughter's relationship though, "What are you doing these days without Markus? I quite liked the boy." Her daughter shifted a little. "Well, I started to write something but I am definitely not showing it to you right now." "Only when you are ready. No hurry." Her mother said unwilling to put any pressure on her daughter. Martha Bates sent Olivia's father an email that night. "Have you seen Olivia lately?"

She got a response from him in the morning. "Why, what's wrong?" "She has lost so much weight. I am worried."

"Maybe she wants to lose weight, it's not such a bad idea." Her husband's email that seemed to signify a casual shrug angered Martha, she wrote back that she was worried and she would appreciate it if he could be a little worried too. This was their daughter.

"I am in San Francisco on Tuesday night, how about we meet up for dinner my love?" She said to her daughter as they both headed to their separate cars.

Olivia didn't know if Stephen was coming on Tuesday, he had said he would confirm on Sunday. She was missing him. His touch, his compliments and he hadn't still seen her in her newer, thinner form, she could feel his fingers running over her, caressing the hollows, kissing them. She didn't know what to call this new version of herself. She hadn't worked toward it on her own volition since she'd never specifically aspired to be thin or thinner as some might say. Fat or for that matter not fat or thin, was all relative, she was beginning to realize. She figured she could always see Stephen after her dinner with her mother should he arrive on Tuesday and agreed to have dinner with her mother.

Stephen came next on Thursday. Olivia was relieved. She hadn't wanted it to coincide with her mother's dinner or her father's, strangely enough because he took her to dinner on Wednesday night. She wondered if it was because her mother had said something to her father, although he did occasionally take her out when he was up in the city.

Kevin looked at his daughter and raised a surprised eyebrow, "Been doing some kind of weight loss thing young lady?" he inquired indulgently. Olivia was always his little girl, there was a touching innocence about her that never grew up he thought. She smiled as she kissed him, "oh well, just getting around the hills of San Francisco, finally." She sighed. Dads weren't as dramatic as moms, thank god!

She wondered what her parents would say if they learned of Stephen. Her father looked younger than Stephen although he was almost sixty.

At 6'2 and broad shouldered, her father would tower over Stephen's 5'8 inch frame for one thing. She didn't think her father would reconcile very easily to her seeing someone a few years younger than him. They'd be so mystified, both her parents, for all their suaveness and progressive thinking, Stephen would come as a shock to them, a major shock, maybe they'd even look at it as a setback that she was settling for on the rebound after her breakup with Markus. If there was anyone she was telling about Stephen it would first be Oliver, her brother. He was the only one who would understand.

He was dating the waitress at the cafeteria next to Harvard and seemed perfectly content with her although he and Olivia had decided they wouldn't tell their parents yet. "Mom and dad are not snobs but Jane's looking to finish up a diploma in catering soon and then she's starting her own business." "Maybe it's best to wait until then?" Olivia agreed. "Lucky for you!" Olivia had said. "At least you don't live here in the thick of things like I do!" This was when she was still engaged to Markus and they were invited to so many parties by both of her parents and Markus's mother that they laughed often at how little time they seemed to have to themselves.

Despite their harmless twittering about their parents, Olivia and Oliver often commented on how lucky they were to have two parents who loved them above all else. It was an unexplained mystery to them as to why their parents got divorced. It was only recently that Martha had bought property in Albuquerque but she often said she could never relinquish her Bay Area connections. Her husband also seemed to still love her very much and anxiously followed her ongoing literary success.

CHAPTER THIRTEEN

The following months comprised of Stephen's more persistent attentions to Olivia and her gradual espousal of small measures she had never before considered regarding her physical appearance. She'd always been the 'oh so cute daughter of Martha Bates." Barring her one childhood incident that was hidden, mostly untouched and what her mother hoped, would remain forever an unawakened trauma. Her life bespoke a happy childhood. She'd been happy with her looks and had stumbled in and out of relationships in college and the years following until she met Markus and her love life had stabilized for a while. Her mother had anxiously watched her graduate through these relationships realizing all this was essential to her eventual maturation.

Martha had been watchfully guarded of her daughter's

relationships but had resisted adroitly the urge to hover around her daughter like helicopter parents did to their college going children.

Stephen began to share some of the work in San Francisco with his team in New York. Anil Rao came down to San Francisco to help him one week. He thought it would be perfect to introduce him to Olivia. He would come across as this lawyer with friends that spanned the ethnic range.. Presenting Anil would show him for the all encompassing lawyer he was and establish the breadth of his contacts, Stephen found himself thinking. Anil had earned his law degree from Harvard and Stephen felt that detail would finely complement the posse of attributes he was assembling to present to Olivia like a carefully picked bouquet. His aim was to continue to impress her and make her comfortable enough to introduce him to her parents, which had yet to happen.

Olivia had steered clear of talk of her parents with Stephen, he was far too shrewd and could figure easily how she felt and didn't think she could handle getting her parents to learn about him just yet. She had no idea what this was, something that happened in the middle of break ups? What was this? She hated to think it but was he just a *hold over* measure? She was still evaluating and simultaneously growing from her experience with Stephen. In her mind she was still unable to accept this as a full-fledged relationship.

When they met at *Trivia* for dinner that night, Stephen had to excuse himself to use the restroom, he'd come straight after finishing a lengthy phone call and had to freshen up he stated.

He introduced Anil and Olivia and left almost immediately although he would have loved to officiate over the introduction but the lobby was extremely crowded and noisy and he excused himself while they waited to be seated. Apparently having reservations at 8 pm didn't mean a whole lot, patrons still ended up waiting. That was a strategy some restaurants employed; keep people waiting so they value you more, so patrons felt especially the blessed reprieve of finally being seated at a table.

They were shown to their table before Stephen returned. Anil felt immediately drawn to Olivia when she handed him her coat and purse to hold as he pulled her chair to help her into her seat. It was such an informal yet intimate gesture and it gave him a tug of pleasure. He was accustomed to Stephen's girls by now. They were often gorgeous beyond belief and impossibly thin. The curious thing about Olivia, Anil thought was that she wasn't impossibly anything. There was an unfussy aura of unawareness around her regarding her looks that made her indescribably appealing to Anil. He looked down at his suit, he'd worn it three days straight and wished he'd changed before coming to dinner. He'd never been this conscious of his clothes he realized with a jolt. He hadn't expected to be captivated by Stephen's girl friend. He knew Stephen often picked some great restaurants and since he wasn't familiar with San Francisco, had agreed to join them when Stephen invited him, purely out of tiredness and the lack of will to find dinner on his own, sheer sloth.

Olivia looked at Anil's card that he handed to her, "How do you say your last name? Is it *Ray oh*?" She pronounced slowly. "No, it rhymes more with cow." "Really?!"

"Phonetically it's difficult to find an equivalent pronunciation in English, I am used to so many variations of pronunciations of my name that it doesn't even occur to me to correct people anymore." "Rao." She said slowly, "Cow, Rao. I get it!" She repeated a few times cheerfully. "Well, that's the closest but indeed you get it." Anil noticed how superb the line of her teeth was when she smiled. Did Stephen know how to pick them or what! He thought with a sigh. He felt an unfamiliar quickening of his pulse.

"Where did you go to school?" "Who me?" He sounded puzzled. He'd been asked that before but not in the first moments of meeting someone socially, maybe at business meetings and such. Olivia was reminded of her first introduction with Stephen and felt it was something everyone in his firm did, announce their college degrees when they met someone new. "Well, I went to the University of Pennsylvania." "Wow. Did you like it there?" She was curious. "Oh, I loved it. In some respects, I think that experience shaped me more than Harvard which I attended later for law school." So he did go to Harvard. She was surprised he didn't tell her that off the bat, like Stephen had with his Yale/Columbia introduction. When Stephen returned he sat next to Olivia and pulled her close to him, "What do you think of my girl Anil?" Anil was completely unprepared for that question and pretended to be immersed in the menu muttering, "What can I say?" "If you haven't eaten here before, you must try their lamb." Olivia offered helpfully, "It's their signature dish." "I could use that, Stephen will pick a good wine I am sure, like he always does." "Thank god I had the presence of mind to get reservations" Stephen observed, taking in the packed restaurant and growing line at the entryway. "I'm sure god had nothing to do with it Stephen, take credit when you can." Anil laughed good-naturedly. "I don't believe in god and all that blah of course." Stephen snorted dismissively.

"You call yourself an atheist then Stephen?" Olivia inquired, picking the smallest piece of bread in the little basket set before them and buttering it ever so lightly, just as Stephen had taught her. "Frankly, I don't spend time dwelling on this." He responded tersely, he turned his attention to a couple that was getting seated, the woman wore a fabulous cream outfit, Anil and Olivia couldn't help following his gaze.

"I can tell you I do Olivia." Anil said, drawing attention back to her question embarrassed at how easily Stephen's attention wandered at the sight of other women.

"Do what?" Stephen edged back into the conversation. "If my belief system or lack of it needs a name, then I have no qualms being dubbed an atheist." He sipped some wine, leaned forward and spoke more reflectively. "All the people I know who are super religious suck. I believe they think believing in god gives them license to be extra bad, like they have someone who can bail them out." "God as insurance?" Olivia laughed merrily, "I love that! Never heard anyone put it quite so clearly before. It's so straightforward if you think of it. That's just it, people feel buoyed by the fact that there is a god they can bribe and compensate when they've behaved badly, versus those who don't believe on the other hand, keep themselves in check, they don't rely on anyone who will come to bail them out, so bad behavior is unbailable to some extent and therefore not manifested.. Does that sound right?"

"A lethal combination of beauty and brains." Anil said raising his glass in a toast to Olivia's summation of his thoughts. Stephen drew her close and kissed her, "my girl" she eased back into her seat not relishing the intimate gesture in front of his colleague whom she'd just met. Anil caught the expression in her eyes as she lowered them to control the rising color in her cheeks. "Sorry." He mouthed, when Stephen bent down to pick up his napkin, he hadn't meant to compliment her so openly in front of her date.

"When I was at Yale, I remember sitting in on a lecture on religion and the woman who was at the podium, can't remember if she was a Professor or some sort of guest speaker but she ended with a proverb that said, "Pray to God, fine; but keep rowing to shore." Stephen laughed heartily at his own comment joining the conversation again with gusto.

"Good one!" Anil agreed laughing as they turned their attention to the waiter who had brought in their dinners. "I didn't mean to make that remark Olivia, religion and politics are taboo subjects, surely at first meetings. I think you put people a little too much at ease, they feel compelled to say anything that comes to their mind."

"Yes but if it's my fault, I am glad for it, it's so nice when people speak their minds Anil." Olivia smiled.

"Awesomely put. That's my girl." Olivia turned to look at her purse to check if her phone was ringing to avoid Stephen making a move to hug and kiss her again in front of Anil. When dinner was done, Stephen hailed a cab for him and Olivia while Anil begged off a ride saying he needed to walk to his hotel after those fabulous lamb chops.

The image of Olivia's bare, ringless hands and perfect teeth, her casual drawing up of her hair at the end of dinner to clip it high above her neck, her unselfconscious manner bore right into Anil's sleep and into his night. He wondered how she got involved with Stephen. It was close to dawn before his eyes closed in sleep still perplexed at his reaction to Olivia. He woke up before the alarm rang, partly because he was on East Coast time and partly because he resolved, through all his tossing and turning to send an email to Olivia.

Olivia saw his email well into her morning at work. Anil had written to her copying Stephen, "Stephen thanks always for a great dinner, even greater company and delectable wine selection. You obviously have immaculate taste. It would be a pleasure to see you again Olivia."

Anil didn't think he could say very much more without incriminating himself as having *fallen* for Olivia? Had he fallen for Olivia? There was nothing he could do about that he'd better snap out of it he thought.

Stephen had been careful not to reveal Olivia's antecedents, that her mother was Martha Bates, the

First Lady of Fiction in America and the rest of the English speaking world, at dinner. That was a trump card he was going to use at a well appointed time at the Christmas party he would take Olivia to, the build up before the unveiling of a rare painting. She still wasn't waif thin as he had wanted her, but the bulges of her curves had smoothened out remarkably as had the looseness that had hung around her arms, dimpled elbows, the double curves at the waist line were all on the wane. The soft, downy aspects of her that had so shocked him when he first ran into her were more compacted. He had held her with possessive pride last night as they exited the restaurant and bid goodbye to Anil.

Given that Anil was unaccustomed to posturing, his reaction to Olivia left Stephen gleeful with self-congratulation. This was what he had been aiming for all along, it was happening again. The girl on his arm was the envy of everyone.

The happy couple headed home as Anil walked alone back to his hotel. Stephen was on the home stretch now he just had a few finishing touches left before Olivia could be made presentation-ready and primed for the unveiling in the few short months before the Christmas party.

CHAPTER FOURTEEN

So much hinged on the Christmas party for Stephen, yes, yes, they called it the Holiday party now but who cared, it was all the same thing, it was the one big event when all the partners showed up with their spouses to mingle with the plebeians in the firm. The firm also recommended people take cabs back home in order to avoid drinking and driving or any other mishap that had the potential to present them in a negative light to the media. Olivia was the absolute centerpiece of his plans, he was orchestrating more than merely basking in the glory by association with Olivia but more because he hoped by then he could announce something that signified permanence in his plans, demonstrating to his colleagues and to senior partners that he should be admitted into the firm's inner sanctums.

It may have occurred to some but the fact had certainly not escaped Stephen's notice that despite his diligent and dogged work with the firm for so long now he was not at a place that he might have been in had he been a properly married partner who had the trappings of a spouse, children, college admissions woes and other things that seemed like the rites of parenting to attest to his overall worth. There was something to be said for people who were married, were they taken more seriously? Given more promotions as an acknowledgement to their commitment? Was Stephen considered frivolous because he was single? Stephen's suspicions lately circled back to the images of all those gorgeous looking women who accompanied him to Christmas parties in the past.

Their office in Manhattan was *the* most influential one in the entire firm but he had always been kept on the fringes of the inner circle, always tantalizingly close but never drawn in. Now, he felt empowered to envision the fruits of his efforts with Olivia coming in the form of: *A*. Getting married to her in rather grand style, perhaps at a romantic Carmel location with Martha Bates and others looking on. *B*. More importantly, get key partners to attend, with perhaps signed and personalized letters of invitation from the Great Bates herself. This could only result in catapulting him to that spot that had eluded him. He wondered at his own miscalculation, for having delayed such an event for so long, he was the shrewd lawyer, the one who knew how to play his cards right, the one who could outsmart so many of his New York colleagues in well, a New York minute.

Here he was within touching distance, kissing distance some might say of sixty that some others seemed to look forward to, for all the rewards they could enjoy but his would come in truncated forms as he would turn sixty without seeing children of his graduate, without being part of that prized selection of people at the top and with the prospects of finding young beauties that much harder as time went by. No matter how much he turned on the charm and how interesting he might appear, his appeal, from now on, would only dwindle. Olivia was fast appearing like a lifeline to him.

His painstakingly nurtured goal. His stagnation at the firm's upper management level without being in the hallowed circle had never loomed in front of him in such large font that seemed potentially able to crush him, it was a menacing picture, it was too sudden and had caught him off guard. Olivia would pry that door of the inner sanctum open for him. Not her, but the what the whole association would imply, place him on that podium level, on par, equal.

He realized also the value in teaming up with Anil who seemed to enjoy very good rapport with some of the top partners, members of that unapproachable circle he was trying to break into. He hoped working with Anil on the new biotechnology giant would give him that edge he desperately felt he needed. Time was playing a sneaky game with him and he had to find a way to out maneuver it. He had been playing hide and seek with signs of aging, dodging mirrors that reflected his shiny head sitting atop often burdened shoulders, his eyes swiftly avoided contact with themselves in the mirror as they didn't want to acknowledge the stoop he seemed to be cultivating, what you don't know can't hurt you, he thought to himself sarcastically as he trudged on.

Stephen was unable to come the following week to attend to his San Francisco client's meeting. He sent Anil instead. "Sorry for making you do this Anil." Stephen loosened his tie tiredly as he spoke to the younger man. Anil shrugged and said he would enjoy being in San Francisco again. "There's talk that the firm might match the size and strength of the San Francisco office with this one, they are talking of increasing the partner count there."

"Huh?" Stephen's eyes narrowed considering the possibilities of that. He was bereft of too much to say at this time, lost in thinking through the implications for him with his firm's further expansion in San Francisco.

Olivia had not responded to Anil's message from a

week ago, neither, he noticed had the email happy Stephen. "Oh well" he thought still feeling he did the right thing in sending a general thank you email message. At the end of his day with the client, he was returning to his hotel and fished out Olivia's business card. She had probably left already, he thought even as he keyed in her phone number, it was nearing eight. He called and got her greeting, *'Thanks for calling Stahlberg, this is Olivia, please leave a message.'*

He left her a message informing her he was in town and had called to say hello and then hesitated and left his cell phone number. At 11 am the next day, his phone rang, it was Olivia, "So how does the New Yorker find himself in San Francisco?"

"Why hello!" "Are you free to grab lunch? I was going to head out early as I have this huge project that will take me through the evening and I am waiting for some more data to come in." "I wish I could, I am at a client right now but can I take a rain check and invite you to dinner tonight instead?" "Well, I am not sure when I'll be done, how about if you call me when you are done with your client and if I am done by then, maybe we can find a place to eat together." Olivia's words stumbled out quickly. He agreed smiling broadly as he put his phone away. The weight of the interminably heavy papers in front of him suddenly got lighter. When he finally stopped at 7:30 pm, he called Olivia anxiously, not sure if she was still at work. "Well, I am still here and will be done in a half hour or so." She sounded tired. "How about dinner then? It will take me about thirty minutes to get back to the city. Tell you what, one of the guys in the office has been raving about this hole in the wall Indian Restaurant somewhere close to your office, do you care for Indian food?"

"Oh yes! I love Indian food!" "I think it's called *'Dil'* I'll email you the address in the next few minutes."

He found out details and emailed them to Olivia. She responded with a smiley face and her cell phone number and a brief, "I should be there around 8:30." He heaved a sigh. At least this place didn't sound like some romantic destination. In fact, he'd been forewarned to ignore the ambience and any grease marks on the tables or walls as it was the food that mattered.

Olivia arrived at about the same time he had, both of them paying off their cabs one behind the other. She was wearing a knee length white shirt held together at the waist with a belt and tight fitting black pants and pumps. He bent forward awkwardly in a half hug greeting. She smiled at him looking at his rolled up sleeves and his jacket slung over his back. He looked refreshingly informal and, she thought for a minute, *exciting?* She couldn't explain the surge she felt upon seeing him again. She liked how he breathed. How could you like how someone breathed, didn't all living things do that? She felt ridiculous and convinced it was a good way of breathing, she liked the movement of his chest and his shoulders, something was surely attractive about him, the hairs on his fingers the firmness of his brown hands.

She had read his email more than once feeling a twinge of expectation at the deliberately restrained tone in it. She hadn't responded because she didn't know what to say in response. Stephen had presented Anil as a *'much junior guy, I'm a mentor to him in a way.'* Stephen had underplayed Anil not just with Olivia but tried to make it seem like he was taking him under his wing even in the office in New York. Anil either didn't seem to notice or care.

"Oh god, my colleague was not kidding, this place is a dive!" Anil was embarrassed as they walked into the restaurant. Stephen wouldn't be caught dead in such a place he thought. He wondered at the wisdom in bringing Olivia to this place. He knew nothing about her, except that she worked for a firm in the city and that she was one of Stephen's many girl friends.

"Well, you can't write it off until you've eaten, so hold your horses." She said putting a hand on him preventing him from backing out of the restaurant. "I don't believe I've eaten here before but if it's this full close to 9:00 on a Wednesday night, they must serve pretty good food." Her firmly optimistic tone put him at ease.

When they were seated at the table an aluminum plate of chopped onions and green chillies slit length ways with slices of lemon was slapped on the table by a guy in a long tunic and loose white pants. They gave their order using the numbers, "We'll have the number 5, 11 and 12 please and two *naans*."

"So you don't speak any Indian?" She asked as he shook his head embarrassed. "Neither Indian nor any of the Indian languages." He smiled. It was her turn to be embarrassed, "Sorry, that sounded quite ignorant didn't it? What is your dialect or mother tongue?" "Telugu." "Tell-u-gu" she repeated after him. He changed the subject and asked her if she worked long hours every day. They ate their food in full concentration and left the restaurant leaving several dollars by way of a tip on the table, fully satisfied with their meal.

"Do you want me to call a cab for you?" He wanted to spend more time with her but wasn't sure what she would say. It was very late his time but he was gradually getting used to the difference, it was his third night in San Francisco. "I have to walk home, after that meal, I'd just better." She said rubbing her stomach.

"Great, I'll walk with you." "Stephen would never

have asked if he could call a cab for me." This was the first time either one of them had brought up Stephen's name that night. Anil wanted to tread cautiously. "Hmmm," he said, waiting for her to clarify. She laughed self-consciously, "You see, I am convinced he wants me to look a certain way and I know he wishes me a lot thinner." Anil felt at a loss for words. It was true that Stephen often seemed to have extremely young and impossibly thin girls hanging on his arm the few times he'd bumped into him in restaurants in New York but he hadn't paid much mind to it.

"Sounds ridiculous, you can't possibly get any thinner." He guided her across the street holding her elbow and let her go when they crossed the street. The warmth of his closeness and the steadiness of his hold did not escape Olivia. She wanted to snuggle into Anil's non-evaluating and stolid presence. She didn't feel the edge that Stephen presented with his constantly vacillating attentions and discussion topics.

He was Stephen's exact opposite in that regard. Stephen was a butterfly, his attention constantly wavering at the sight of pretty faces and tight bottoms. He was also continuously gauging the reactions of others to them, assessing how the two of them appeared to others, evaluating reactions from people. He was the most distracted person she knew. She was realizing how much a victim to appearances he was on every level. Anil was practically oblivious of everyone around him except her and was deeply focused on their conversation. They had ordered exactly what each one wanted without so much as a mind to calorie counts or ramifications on the bathroom scale. They talked about their common love of films, books, their undergraduate college experiences. She felt she'd covered more ground with Anil about her youth during that dinner than she'd done with Stephen in all the months she'd known him.

After they'd walked for more than an hour Anil said, "Are we anywhere near your home?" Olivia laughed heartily, "I'm leading you astray!" "You are." Anil replied gravely. She didn't want to acknowledge his meaning and pointed in the uphill direction to her left, "I am up a few blocks that way. I'd invite you in for coffee or tea but it's Wednesday and both of us have to work tomorrow."

"Absolutely! I'll try and get a cab back to my hotel." She leaned forward and gave him a hug bidding him goodnight. He felt a rush of warmth at the touch of her softness as she leaned against him for an instant. He gave her shoulder a little squeeze and let her go quickly afraid of his need to hold on to her. She was his colleague's girl friend, he had to be careful, it wouldn't do to be helping himself to treats he wasn't entitled to.

Anil walked back to his hotel failing to find a cab. His

sleep had drifted away making room for his thoughts to fully shape themselves in his head like animated stories moving fast forward and rewinding.

Anil's last serious girl friend had been a petite Asian named Tracy who dressed in layers of sweaters. They had met at Harvard and had been together for almost three years. Their families also had met and become friends expecting the eventual to happen but Tracy had started seeing someone at work when Anil was traveling frequently to Washington D.C. and often had to spend weeks in D.C. His aim had been to establish himself enough and see if Tracy could find something interesting for herself in the nation's capital. Maybe she didn't want to move to D.C, he never found out, she wrote him a lengthy letter full of sobs and pictures of their time together telling him it was over for her and she had emotionally "transitioned."

It took him close to a year to digest that break up. He got used to using his work as a rehab tool, delving into every difficult project that came by and abandoning any thought of socializing. After fourteen months or so he spent one Thanksgiving at his colleague Brian's home and was introduced to his cousin Laura who became so fond of Anil, she told him bluntly that she considered him a worthwhile enough person to move to the city for from Bethesda. He cautioned her that it was still very early days and he didn't know if he was fully ready to contemplate a new relationship yet.

Whether Laura had wanted the relationship with Anil or a reason to move from a familiar and boring family to D.C, Anil never found out, having striven throughout the relationship to dissuade her from taking the whole thing seriously he had to break it off eventually. Laura seemed like she wanted out of her life of privilege, pomp and circumstance. She saw in Anil a chance to be absorbed into a whole different world, it was that vision that she conjured up that had propelled her more than anything he had done to seduce her into a relationship. The basis for their union had been far too flimsy to survive the test of time not to mention Anil's rigorous work schedules. Six months into moving to D.C., to be close to Anil, Laura returned to her parents' enormous home in Bethesda, summarily dismissing all things 'exotic.'

Anil found the opportunity at Jones & Boyle a few months later and left D.C. for New York realizing the cultural acclimatization this would take on his part in terms of the work environments, not just in terms of the culture of the new firm but also the industries he would be focusing on.

He entered and exited trains and subways gingerly bracing himself to run into Tracy, the girl he almost married, the girl who left him without too much of an explanation. He smarted at the fact that it still bothered him so much. He was very wary of the tumult of feelings he was experiencing with Olivia. The only uncomplicated aspect of this was how unambiguously attracted to her he was. Everything else was a mess. *I mean*, he thought helplessly, *she is Stephen's girl friend, this is pilfering!* Despite all his loud mannerisms, Stephen was a nice fella and who was Anil to judge his right to find a girl like Olivia? For the first time, he didn't think of Tracy when he was with Olivia. To him that was the most liberating part of Olivia. He realized that he hadn't thought of Tracy in fact since he first met Olivia. She'd functioned as a nicotine patch that exorcised all remaining traces of Tracy.

Olivia went home thinking she hadn't been so involved in what someone was saying or thinking or feeling at any time. She had not felt that with Markus certainly. With Stephen she had felt spurred to a challenge, to do more, almost to perform a dance to an unsung melody he had constructed for her. She found the intensity of Anil's dark brown eyes mesmerizing as he listened to her speak as he watched her, aware that he was aware of her every pore. She knew it was useless to try and deny that.

From the beginning she'd had trepidation of that with Stephen, that she was contorting her person to be something else. She went home thinking of sending an email to Anil thanking him for dinner and waited up to see if he would respond, she finally dozed off.

Anil steered clear of Olivia for the rest of his trip. He left for New York steeling himself against the urge to respond to Olivia or to call her. He spent the remaining two nights working well past 9pm so he would have no time to think of calling her. Two days later when the announcement came to turn off cell phones and pagers before the plane was to take off, he eagerly turned off his phone. Now he wouldn't have to fight that urge to call Olivia, with the phone so readily tingling in his hand.

He tried to quell the yearning to want to hear her voice, to hear the catch of her breath when her voice dropped conspiratorially when she wanted to say something obnoxious and did not want to be overheard. He found that quality so irresistible when she dropped her voice to a hush and talked in breathy whispers as they walked aimlessly about for over an hour after their dinner, like she was afraid she might offend someone if they should overhear anything controversial she could be saying. There was no one around for several blocks! It showed how wary she was of giving offence in anyway.

This was too much of an entanglement and although he had sensed corresponding vibes from Olivia all through the evening, he could not read into it more than a natural friendliness she was capable of that was perhaps her general nature and had nothing to do with him, plus she was Stephen's girl friend, wasn't she?

He fell back into his seat and closed his eyes, refusing the drink and snack service, just waiting to be swallowed up by work when he got into New York.

CHAPTER FIFTEEN

It was funny how he and Stephen got out of their respective cabs at the exact same time on Monday morning outside their New York office. He didn't get a chance to prepare himself and looked down at Stephen with a wide grin, "hello!"

Stephen juggled his bag and his coat, it was a warm day, "Heard you guys went to a phenomenal Indian restaurant last week!" He sounded excited.

"Well, I wouldn't call it phenomenal, it was a very modest place but with some great, if spicy Indian food."

"That's something I need to warm up to, do they serve good wines at these places?" "Actually, we had smuggled in beers from a liquor store next door, the restaurant doesn't have a liquor license."

"Beer eh?" Stephen's brow furrowed. He wasn't sure if Olivia should be consuming any beer. He wanted to ask Anil how many beers she'd had but withheld his questioning as they entered the elevator and the chatter shifted to other subjects to include the other colleagues riding up with them.

Anil realized with a start that the only way Stephen would have known that he'd been to an Indian restaurant was through Olivia. They hadn't talked after that night and he was not aware what he was supposed to say or not say but decided he'd let Stephen bring up the discussion. He wondered what Olivia made of his silence to her email. He wished he'd responded, now it would be so much harder to reconnect, even if for purely social reasons. He did have to travel back to the San Francisco client often and she was among the two or three people he knew there.

Stephen came breezily into Anil's office later that morning. "Guess what?! Olivia's going to be in New York for a Private Equity meeting next week. Isn't it such great luck we don't have to be in San Francisco then?"

Anil was startled at the excitement he felt. He was immensely grateful for being dark enough to be able to conceal his flush of anticipation. Olivia in New York? But Stephen would probably be her primary tour guide and companion. What reason would *he* have to connect with her? He should have written to her in response to her email. It was an innocuous note acknowledging a good evening and great food. It's quite likely she had felt rebuffed at his lack of response. It's possible that she loved Stephen and looked to making a friend in Anil, no more.

Anil wished he could find reason to be in San Francisco when Olivia was in New York. He felt the gaucheness of his demeanor shining through like a highlighted reprimand.

He didn't get to dwell on Olivia or anything being sucked into an enormous case they were working on that kept him working through the weekend and into midnight on Monday. On Tuesday, he strode into work at close to eleven in the morning. He stopped short on his tracks when he saw Olivia standing in the lobby, she saw him and waved, moving forward to greet him. She gave him a hug and he was still too startled to do more than hug her back. "Stephen isn't picking up his phone, I am here for a conference that is on Wednesday and Thursday." She spoke very quickly joining words together that she hoped connected and made sense.

Anil took her by her elbow and led her to a sofa at the far end of the lobby away from the reception desk. "Stephen did mention you were going to be here." "So you knew I was coming?" Olivia asked him, looking at him squarely. "Yes. Stephen seemed very happy that you were visiting."

Olivia looked at him and felt the warmth of his agitated feelings fan against her. She realized how captive he was to the fact that she was Stephen's girl friend and that he couldn't encroach. How decent. She saw how happy he was to see her and how conflicted at the same time. She wore a grey wool dress that landed above her knees, her stockinged legs disappeared into boots that reached her knees. She couldn't be more perfect he thought. His eyes eagerly taking in her beautiful coat and orange and gray silk scarf tucked into a dark blue coat. She was stunning. "You look wonderful." He couldn't help himself. "Thank you!" She impulsively blurted out, "It's all due to Stephen!" "What is all due to Stephen?" Anil was puzzled. "Anil!" She sighed. "I was Project Olivia!" *"Project Olivia!?"* He was even more confounded. "Aren't you his girl friend?" "I am." She looked so crestfallen at the question and for having to respond that she sat completely silent.

Anil's customarily easy demeanor felt like it was churning with so many unasked questions that he remained silent. "Anil, would you have asked me out if I had not been one of Stephen's girls?" He never got to respond. Stephen was suddenly in their midst, they hadn't seen him enter the lobby and the security person pointing Stephen to his waiting guest. Stephen enveloped Olivia into a bear hug, kissing her and turning brightly to Anil. "Thanks pal for taking care of my girl." Olivia looked down. "My pleasure." Anil said as he made to leave with an inclusive goodbye to the two of them.

"My, my, look at you!" Stephen said, holding Olivia at arm's length, taking in the entire look. "Have you lost more weight?" His question came with a lilt of expectation that he was right.

"I lost close to fifty pounds using *La Methode Baylor*, if you must know Stephen." "No, you can't be serious!" Stephen exclaimed in genuine surprise. "You didn't have that much to lose!"

"Well I did and thanks to you, I am not getting it back." She laughed as she sat back on the sofa. "*La Methode Baylor* does have commercial potential I am convinced, you should try marketing it." Stephen glanced at her to see if he was right in detecting a certain terseness or sarcasm in her tone. Whatever it was, was uncharacteristic of her. He shook his head nonplussed. "Listen, Beautiful, I have to march off you know, drudgery calls amidst this temptation to spend time with you."

"Oh stop it!" She exclaimed angrily. "You..." her voice broke off as her cell phone started to ring in her purse. She glanced at the number and answered the phone. "Yes Pete, I got in very late yesterday. I can meet you for lunch, sure, I'll be there at 12:30 and we can go over stuff."

Stephen wasn't sure what Olivia was about to say. She turned around and left abruptly. He couldn't tell what had come over her. Olivia hurried out and stopped a cab. "The Waldorf please." She got off and ran up to her hotel room to change into slacks and a sweater. She suddenly felt her dress was too 'evening' for work. She dashed out and ran the few steps to St. Bart's, where she was to meet Pete for lunch. She was still simmering under the exchange she had on the way into New York with the woman sitting next to her on the plane.

The Private Equity conference Olivia was to attend wasn't beginning until Wednesday. She had told Stephen she would be arriving on Tuesday night but had changed her plans after talking with Oliver who said he would be able to take her to dinner on Tuesday night and she arrived a day earlier, clearing it with her boss who gave her some files and asked her to meet with Pete, a partner in Stahlberg's New York office and help him out on Tuesday. Pete had reached out to Olivia's boss telling him he needed to finish up a presentation he was working on to present to a European client. Olivia was happy to help, she had all the data they would need to craft the message. All of the firm's marketing materials and competitive information was available on the intranet anyway.

Plus, she would enjoy a few days at the fabulous Waldorf Hotel.

She wrote to Stephen informing him she would be arriving on Tuesday but hadn't notified him of her change of plans about arriving a day earlier. She had yet to see any response from Anil to her email thanking him for dinner at *Dil*. Funny, she thought. She couldn't remember when she'd enjoyed a meal with someone more. She had never felt more natural with another man, it felt like it did when she was with Mother and Oliver and Father but was buoyed by the feeling of reciprocal comfort. Anil's amazing smile, the stubborn lock of hair that fell forward on his forehead that caused his eye to twitch every so often. His unplanned, intimate touches, at her elbow, on her shoulder as he guided her on the sidewalks. She had felt a thrill and had wanted to snuggle into that sensation. It felt so, she couldn't find another word for it, *so natural*. Stephen was never this spontaneous. She shook her head impatiently, why was she comparing the two?

Not only did she find Anil physically attractive and charming, she was drawn to his unpretentious nature. More drawn to him because he wasn't questing, searching or calibrating. Oddly enough, she felt at home with him, like they'd grown up together and knew each other's childhood haunts. He hadn't so much as hugged her for Christ's sake! She thought with an embarrassed laugh. At the end of each encounter with Stephen she was left wondering if he had gotten what he had been seeking, there was something beseeching about his demeanor, like he was on a jaded treasure hunt. She had sensed a mixture of fatigue and disenchantment with his job and his life, all of which got an uplift when he felt enthralled with the possibilities of being with her, of being catapulted out of near oblivion to basking in some element of stardom and celebrity. Stephen felt the conspiracy of Time moving past him in Stealthy Glee but was heartened as he could see his moment in the sun coming, Olivia was it. No matter where he looked, he couldn't find anyone close to her in value, allure and reach. She was certainly the brightest star in his 'girldex' as he'd come to laughingly dub his rolodex of girlfriends, current, concurrent and past.

After her lunch with Pete, she agreed to edit the presentation they'd identified would work for his meeting with the European company and she promised to send him a draft to review by 4pm. "I should be able to work on it tonight Pete, I am on California time, so I will not be able to sleep early anyway." Pete smiled back at her, "Thank you Olivia." He was surprised he'd never noticed how startlingly pretty the girl was before when he'd visited the San Francisco offices. She seemed to have etched quite a personality out for herself.

Olivia was meeting Oliver later that night. She could talk with him about what she'd uncovered on her flight into New York. She was sure Oliver would be able to advise her. Oliver and Markus had gotten along famously. Her brother had been quite confused when she had broken off her engagement with Markus. Now she would have to spill the beans to Oliver on Stephen, explain her transformation from her plump, sweet self to becoming this magnificent swan and also let him know how Stephen had perhaps intended to use her. What hurt her the most was that he probably had never really loved her. He had loved the thought of changing her, the challenge she offered in her migration from being a comfortable comely girl to a sensational and fashion conscious diva.

More than anyone else's reaction, it was Oliver's that made her the happiest. "What on earth have you gone and done Via?" Her brother lifted her off her feet as he enveloped her in a hug. "I would *never* have been able to do this before!"

"Stop being nasty Oliver!" She exclaimed happily. "Is it really that dramatic?!" She asked. Despite her welling self-loathing and rising resentment toward Stephen, she couldn't shake off the underlying gratitude she felt for him. He had literally peeled away at the layers that she had been shrouded under. Made her a more flirtatious person even. She started to respond to the responsiveness her new self created, baffled as she was by the fact that shaving off forty or fifty pounds should suddenly make her more visible and not less.

She recalled how he'd introduced her to the Filbert Steps in San Francisco, rising up from Sansome Street to the Coit Tower. Really? She had to be made aware by a self-professed New Yorker about widely known San Francisco haunts, jaunts, hikes and walks? Turned out he had a wonderful reference book on hidden walking paths of San Francisco that he'd used as a guide. That Stephen, with his tucked bag weighing him down on one side, yes, he carried everything, his computer and printer and various files he was working on. She couldn't but be impressed. She didn't know if her mother had similar fetishes about safeguarding her work. Maybe in a litigious environment you could never be too careful.

Olivia had made it a practice to run up Filbert Steps twice a week before walking home. If someone had said to her just six months ago that she was capable of so much rigorous exercise she would have scoffed at their audacity to even suggest such a thing. No one would have said that to her. Her parents treated her almost too gently and were the most uncritical parents one could hope for. Was that good or bad? Was her incentive only to be held by Stephen as he ran his hands over her body exclaiming over the newly created hollows, bending down to kiss the definite curve of her waist as it fanned gently into sloping hips. How could she not recognize the fact as to what Stephen actually cared about? He'd given her alternate steps to run up should she tire of the Filbert Steps, Greenwich Street Stairs for instance. He was always careful to extricate the sting from his proposals. It was the weirdest thing to be wooed in such a manner. He must find her appealing in some way? Mustn't he?

But her face went hot and she looked away uncomfortably from the mirror not wanting to see her eyes reflect the tortured introspection she was going through. She would meet Oliver and things would be better. She recalled what her mother had said several years ago about developing the characters in her novels. *Imagine others without your consciousness*, Martha Bates had said, *imagine them without your id spinning down the spine of what constitutes them and that let's you see others for what they are minus what you are. Because honey, think about it, regardless of you, their lives are quite complete so there has to be that separation that allows you to objectify to some extent.* She wondered why she recalled her mother's comment.

Was this her way of finding an excuse for Stephen or a way of excusing herself? Was it just childish folly that had allowed her to become so wrapped up with a man who was clearly dotted with question marks? She started when she thought of Uncle Paul. Her chest heaved as she backed off from that memory. She shuddered and sat at the edge of the bed. Why did his face come into her mind now? Uncle Paul was going to help her spell Madeleine, Stephen was showing her how to lose weight. It was important not to misspell Madeleine, it was important to be thin, the way Stephen wanted her. She'd trusted Uncle Paul to help her so she could pull off her party in fine form. She wished she could take that memory and toss it under the train and let it be swallowed up under the weight of the tracks, instead her mother's book had gone into the tracks, she'd never worked on retrieving it, knowing her mother would always be able to sign another copy for her. What had she written in that book? Olivia could vaguely recall, "Darling, a deep breath as you enter the world on your own, indulge in the good stuff, skirt the bad and don't dwell on things that bring you pain. The pursuit of happiness is yes, that simple."

Olivia remembered that her mother had been agitated all day at her graduation. She seemed nervous and unsettled. Olivia felt an unfamiliar squeamishness clamming her vocal chords. "Can you write something for me in my book mom?" Mother and daughter had looked at each other. Olivia was graduating from high school and neither of them had ever talked about that incident with Uncle Paul. Olivia understood the cacophony of action that had followed the news of Uncle Paul's sudden death. She wondered often if she had been the reason for her parents' breaking up but had been so smothered with attention and love from both of them that she'd never examined that suspicion. It wasn't just the conversation on the plane with Moira heading into JFK that had upended her feelings for Stephen. It was also this connection that had loomed itself between Uncle Paul, the benevolent kindness of his look, his ready open arms echoed Stephen's incessant praise and endless efforts to move to the next level, whether it was to help her lose more weight or edge closer to her parents and all that portended for him in some way.

She got up, changed again into her gray dress and headed out to her dinner with Oliver. She needed so badly to talk with him. Her wonderfully calm brother who pored over books with unflinching attention. Now she needed his unflinching attention. He needed to focus on her like she was The Iliad.

Oliver had a surprise for her. He'd brought Jane to meet his sister. Olivia was startled but delighted to finally meet Jane. "She somehow managed to have this one night off for the next several nights and we decided to come out together to see you." Jane gave Olivia a hug before sitting down, "Three over worked people! Boy, do we need something to drown our sorrows in?" She laughed merrily as she passed the wine list to Olivia. Olivia felt immediately at ease with Oliver's girl. She was a sturdy brunette with a lilting laugh and gusto for food and words, sharing her ample information of the ingredients and origins of the dishes with charming anecdotes.

Jane recommended their entrée selections and ordered the wine. "I hope I haven't gotten ahead of myself." "No way!" Olivia exclaimed, "None of us in our family knows how to cook, we really aren't that into cooking. Surprising! Given how much we are into eating!" Oliver laughed. "Yeah, I knew Jane was going to be my life saver there!"

"You don't look very much like the picture your brother has of you in his apartment." Jane said as they sat back after a supersized meal. "She looks positively emaciated." Oliver clicked away, "Now that's a good imitation of what Grandma would say." Olivia grimaced at her brother.

Jane sat back in her chair to appraise Olivia better, "I don't know what you looked like before but I must say your brother's right about how stunning you look. I don't believe it's an ugly duckling to swan story however, I'm pretty sure you had all the main ingredients for beauty to begin with." Olivia reached forward and gave Jane a warm squeeze on her arm.

Olivia could tell why Oliver was so smitten and quite possibly completely in love with Jane. Jane was the same age as him but seemed to have accumulated so much experience. She'd lived in Italy and in South Africa. She'd traveled to South America, Mexico and extensively in North America. Her family of five doted on each other, despite the freedom they'd had to explore, travel and regroup, the chips always fell within the same geography. Her father was a diplomat in Washington and her mother designed greeting cards that she sold to various retail outlets.

Her brothers, both younger than Jane were employed in Philadelphia and New York. The family met fairly frequently and there was a merry-go-round of fluid conversations and exchange of information where they all stayed abreast of each other's whereabouts. "Nope, we aren't Facebook friends anymore and but we've kept our Yahoo groups page. We cherish what we have though, I know it's not common." Jane said, her face pink and eager with excitement as she recounted her stories.

Oliver held her hand throughout the evening. Olivia was deeply comforted he had found someone like Jane. He'd been engaged to a classmate earlier in his early twenties, but their mutual academic calendars fraught with assignments and deadlines drove them asunder. He'd dated relentlessly after that and found that he was attracted to most women who could smile and engage him, but none of those ventures had panned out until now.

He'd met Jane at a colleague's party. She had been catering the event there. He had put one little spinach and brie artichoke heart into his mouth and had reached out for another before the tray went moving and Jane stopped to let him help himself to more. "I'll say, that's a compliment." Oliver noted her auburn hair and dark, smiling eyes, her crisp white shirt over a short black skirt and stockinged feet in Babydoll high-heeled shoes. He ate three more as he talked with her and she enlightened him about what she was serving up for dinner and maybe he should hold off on wolfing the appetizers down so he could leave room for the cod she was serving that night.

When Oliver had talked with Olivia after the dinner a few days later he still felt the memory of satisfaction of having eaten a fabulous meal. By the end of that evening he told Olivia that he had seen more of Jane than of any of his colleagues or of his host for that matter. He'd asked her to go to dinner with him and she told him she wasn't free for the next five nights and that she would call if she got freed up.

Oliver was pleasantly surprised to find her voice on his message machine when he checked it a few nights later. Yes, she could do dinner on Thursday, if he was still free that is. He waited for Thursday like a school kid waiting for game day.

Consequent to their wonderful dinner and Oliver's introducing Jane to her, Olivia's eye opening experience on the plane the night before had been left unmentioned. She couldn't possibly bring up the subject when meeting Jane for the first time. Although, she felt she could at some point relate her experience to Jane. She felt a bond with her like she'd felt with Anil. She could consider telling him things she wouldn't share with Stephen. She felt an uprising of anger at herself and a revolt against both men, although she had no idea why she should feel any anger against Anil. It was Stephen who had this magnum plan all plotted out for a Christmas party denouement.

She was still amazed at how accidental the whole thing was and how she would have allowed herself to wallow in the pleasure of being in Stephen's arms, despite her mind having frequently drifted to dwelling on Anil since their dinner all those weeks ago. She kept recalling the pressure of Anil's hand pulling her back firmly as she stumbled on the uneven climb uphill in her high heels after their dinner that night in San Francisco. She hadn't wanted to change into her walking shoes, she wanted to look tall and gainly for Anil. How light she felt against his strength and the tug she'd felt at his pull. She couldn't ever recall wanting to be *ensconced*, was that the right word? quite so completely. Her brow furrowed at how selective she was getting lately with trying to identify how she really felt about Stephen versus her feelings for Anil, like filleting bone from fish.

Was she being too eager to embrace this newly found information without evaluating it very much? She sat down finally to confront what had happened on the flight into JFK. She had the aisle seat, the woman sitting to her left in the middle seat kept hugging herself as they took off and Olivia had turned to her sympathetically, "I know, they don't give out blankets anymore." She felt bad she couldn't offer her anything, she was clad in a warm sweatshirt and yoga pants, her normal travel wear, but new. She'd pretty much gotten herself a new wardrobe with her drastic loss in weight.

As soon as the captain had turned off the seat belt sign the woman asked Olivia if she could pull out her sweatshirt from the overhead bin. Olivia got up to give it to her and as she handed it noticed the emblazoned logo of Stephen's law firm, Jones & Boyle, the lines of the J&B joined on the top with the Jones & Boyle below. She exclaimed, "I know someone who works there!" She exclaimed, handing the sweatshirt to the woman.

"You are kidding me! Who?" The woman asked. "Well, Stephen Baylor." Olivia was suddenly conscious wondering how she would explain what Stephen was to her. "Oh." The one word Olivia got from the woman piqued her curiosity. "Do you work there as well?" The woman nodded. "Have you heard of him?" "Well, everyone's heard of Stephen!" The woman gave a little laugh that didn't seem to say much but left the door open for much interpretation. "Do you have clients in San Francisco as well?" Olivia asked the woman, hoping to coax her out of her reticence. "No, no, no!" the woman exclaimed. Olivia introduced herself. "I'm Olivia." "Hi, I'm Moira. So you live in New York or in San Francisco?" The woman asked her shaking hands briefly with Olivia. "Oh, I'm from here, just flying to New York on some work." "I am not a lawyer, just part of the support staff. I support some of the partners, not Stephen. I was out here for a friend's wedding in Napa." Moira said. "Oh how nice!" "Yes, it was great, we grew up together in Philadelphia."

"How long have you been with the firm?" Olivia wanted to learn more about Stephen, prompted more now by the tone in Moira's voice. "Well, it will be eight years next July." Moira said with a sigh. Olivia leaned back in her seat and pulled off the clip that held her hair.

"Nice hair! Are you Stephen's new girl!" Moira's unchecked remark made Olivia sit up straight. "How do you mean?" "Oh, it's just that Stephen's always brings the best looking girls to the company Christmas parties." She gave Olivia a well-meaning smile, "like you."

Suddenly Olivia felt a strong urge to confide in Moira.

Nice, Moira with her blonde hair cut squarely at her chin, her brown eyes atop freckled cheeks showing honesty. Olivia thought Moira must be around sixty. Her friend sure married quite late, it could mean so many things Olivia thought. It could be the first or the fourth wedding, anything was possible these days. Why, if either one of her parents decided to marry now, they would be getting married quite late in life.

"I hope you are not cross Olivia. Stephen's a nice guy and all, I don't have much to do with him and I know his secretary Shawna loves him but he is known to have a roving eye, that guy. Gorgeous girls though, all of them. Wonder how he does it, I could carry one of Stephen's girls in my arm and walk across Manhattan, they are often that light." Moira's smiling eyes softened her remarks.

Olivia smiled and pursed her lips ruefully. She didn't want to foster a conversation about Stephen like this, out of the blue, the actual blue sky, if you come to think of it she thought. Moira's recounting of Stephen's various 'Christmas girlfriends' as she called them only confirmed what Olivia had somewhat suspected in the back of her mind all along. Stephen just loved women, just many of them and perhaps simultaneously. Plus they all were made to order, to *Stephen Baylor's Specific Measurements*. Her face flushed with the insult she felt.

So now Olivia was in a 'grooming period' the fattening of the calf before the slaughter at the Christmas Party? She didn't feel gullible or stupid, just insulted for no reason. How could she be found guilty if a burglar decided to burglarize her home coming down the pipes outside a fully secured balcony, if she had been mindful enough to lock her front door?

When she awoke before the flight was about to land, Moira was still asleep. In the scramble to deplane, neither woman exchanged information. Moira bade Olivia a cheerful goodbye, "We left late but we didn't arrive late, that's good!" She said yawning taking her own time getting up and a guy behind them wedged himself in between and the two women dispersed in the ensuing rush of passengers to disembark.

When Olivia got back to her hotel she noticed she'd missed three calls from Stephen and one from another 212 number that she didn't recognize. She listened to her messages from Stephen, "So how is New York treating a Gorgeous San Franciscan?!" and then, "How is my Bombshell doing?" Capping off with the third message, a faint note of irritation seeping in, "I must say Beauties are hard to track down these days?" Olivia hadn't explained what she was doing that night, that she had had plans with Oliver.

The fourth message was from Anil. "Olivia, answer to your question, yes, I would have asked you out if you weren't my colleague's girlfriend. Here's my number, give me a call if you need anything." He proceeded to leave her his phone number.

Olivia stared at her phone and replayed Anil's message before saving it. He was so damned direct and honest, she thought irritably.

She went to her computer and started to work on the presentation for Pete, working well past midnight until 1 am. She felt she had to talk with Stephen, she was angry and was probably imagining worse things about him than were warranted. She finally wrote out an email and studied the draft over and over.

"Stephen, I am not sure I care to be groomed to be your 'Christmas Party Companion.' I owe my newfound confidence to you perhaps but something tells me it wasn't just me that had interested you. I was looking forward to this trip but now I wish I'd never come. But, if I'd never come, I'd never have known."

Olivia

Olivia saved the draft without sending it. Her mother had said to her long ago, "When you are mad with someone, write that email but don't hit send until you've had a chance to sleep over it. That way you get it out of your system and can decide what to do in the light of day." Olivia had offered some tart response to her mother then but somehow allowed herself to be cautioned by that advice now. She was at least able to fall asleep. Waking up the next morning was a struggle, "Oh no!" She muttered when she saw the time. She barely had time to get showered. She fled to the conference and stayed busy all day.

She'd been on her feet and she noticed that her new, lighter self didn't seem to need to eat that often nor did it need to rest that often. She couldn't help feeling a rush of guilt and gratitude toward Stephen. No matter what, he was instrumental in her caterpillar to butterfly transformation.

She wondered at that. Would Anil or anyone else who reacted to her the way they did or have felt the same way had it not been for her new self? She had to talk with Oliver. She hated how busy their lives were. She sent her brother an email, "Oliver, I need to talk with you, there's a conference dinner tonight that I can skip maybe, can you meet me somewhere if you are still in the city?" She heard from Oliver hours later when her feet were killing her and she was flushed with so many conversations, feeling exhausted and hungry but unable to eat. She looked at Oliver's response. "I am back at the college, we returned this morning Via. Can we talk on the phone after your dinner?"

She finally found herself enjoying dinner with some East Coast colleagues and left a little before 9. She hurried up to her hotel room and undressed and slipped into bed to dial Oliver's number. "Hello, hello, is everything okay?" Oliver's voice hinted at the quizzical smile in his voice.

"Hmmm, I don't know Oliver." "How long has it been since you've seen Markus?" She sighed. Markus seemed so long ago and her family seemed unable to think past him. That's because they hadn't met Stephen and she hadn't mentioned him to anyone. They all assumed she'd lost weight so drastically following her break up with Markus. "No, no! How much time do you have to talk?" She asked him, glancing at her watch, it was after 9:30. "Well, we got in real late last night and although I don't see Jane again until Friday, I have some stuff to do. But what is it?" "It's not Markus, Oliver." And she proceeded to tell him as briefly as she could what had happened. "So let's get this straight Via. Somehow you feel you owe this Stephen bloke either yourself as you are now or you think it will make you feel better if you went back and gained the forty or fifty odd pounds that way you don't owe him anything and that would justify your turning him down?"

"Gosh, Oliver!" Olivia laughed brightly but that was exactly how she had felt all day. Like she should wear a fat cloak around her and then it would embolden her to confront Stephen, look into his beseeching watery eyes and tell him she didn't care for his plotting and planning, she wasn't going to be his guinea pig anymore.

CHAPTER SIXTEEN

She didn't mention Anil or bring him up because she was still confused about her feelings for him and that wasn't the issue in any case. The issue was how she might sequester herself from Stephen's enormous influence. She looked at herself lying in bed, the bathrobe from the hotel had slipped to reveal her stomach and she felt a tinge of guilt at how flat it appeared as she straightened the robe to cover her stomach. "From what you tell me Via, I think this guy was gunning for more than a slim you, looks like he saw you as some prize catch because of whose daughter you are." He stopped short, "Gosh I am such a louse, of course he may have been attracted to you for you, don't get me wrong but this whole account I am hearing makes me wonder at the sincerity behind the fellow's intentions."

Olivia gasped but didn't say anything. She heard Oliver stifle a yawn, "Sorry dear, it's almost 10:15! We can talk later, go to bed now." She lay awake thinking of what Oliver said.

It wasn't even just a slimmer her, it was a very thin Olivia combined with the fact that she was Martha Bates' daughter. How could Olivia not have seen that? At two in the morning, when she got up to get a drink of water she opened her computer and saw the draft sitting in her email and she didn't think it said what she wanted it to say.

She wasn't sure what she wanted to say. Oliver was quite astute but she couldn't bear to think of her entire 'Stephen Encounter' having been such a micromanaged charade. She sent him an email that didn't say much, by now he was expecting something from her and she owed him a response. She wrote, "Stephen, Please stop calling me." She started to type that she didn't wish to see him anymore but deleted everything else, left it at that one line, signed her name and sent it off. Almost instantly her phone rang, it was Stephen. She turned off her phone and flipped through a magazine that the Hotel had provided.

In the morning she awoke to an email from Stephen, "Olivia, *(Finally! He'd called her by her name!)* "Are you upset about something honey? We can meet and talk about it. Don't worry. Work can be stressful, trust me I know!" How clever! Olivia thought sarcastically. She went off to work and called a cab later in the afternoon to take her to the airport.

Amidst all this, the only wise thing she felt she'd done was not write back to Anil or respond to his voice mail. She'd saved his message and had listened to it a few times. She'd also saved his phone number but couldn't bring herself to call either one of them.

Stephen wondered how he was going to get the *Baylor Plan* back on track. The following week he had to go to Denver. He met up with Emma Joy over dinner. She seemed mellow and chastened by something. It was so nice to have her not be a prima donna. She could be quite entertaining when she got off her high horse. Someone has let her down badly Stephen thought as he watched what he thought was a quiet behind her eyes, noted the softness of her speech and how she placed her hand on his at the restaurant.

"I missed you Stephen." She smiled softly. He gave her hand a squeeze. She was his back up girl and for some reason he felt he was her back up guy come back to save her. Something must have happened with whoever it was she was reaching up to, she looked censured and cut down to size. Even her clothes didn't project her as flamboyantly and assertively as she normally liked to appear. Her sweater and slacks were far more muted although given her svelte figure, heads turned anyway to look at her, her striking height and fetching cheekbones garnering attention.

He looked around him and glanced at women sitting in the restaurant. Emma Joy was really a showpiece by comparison, there was no question. Yes, her pedigree sucked and she had almost nothing fancy in terms of academic credentials but she'd have to do at least for now, until things got resolved with Olivia. He was determined to make that happen. His eyes narrowed when he thought of how he'd transformed her. What he wouldn't have given to have met Martha Bates!

Stephen and Anil made it back to San Francisco again in three weeks. Anil sensed there was something the matter between Olivia and Stephen but was not going to inquire of course. "I will take Olivia out to dinner tonight, catch you in the morning Anil!" Stephen said casually. Anil couldn't tell how authentic Stephen's statement was. He went to *Dil* and ate the same things he had ordered with Olivia. He looked at the crowded place filled with European tourists, Indians, Pakistanis and marveled at the mix of patrons the restaurant enjoyed.

Stephen called Olivia at work from the office number at his firm. "Hello" "Olivia, it's Stephen, please don't hang up. Listen, can I take you out to dinner?" "I have my book club meeting tonight." She responded. "Tomorrow night then please?" She sighed. She knew she had to see him to confront him with all her suspicions.

"I can do lunch tomorrow." She said, "Why don't we grab a sandwich and walk on the Embarcadero?" Stephen had a lunch meeting with Fenton planned but felt it was far more important to resolve issues with Olivia. Screw Fenton. "Okay sweetie, I can't wait to see you." His optimism kicked in again, with so little encouragement, 'gosh what a Pollyanna!' she thought irritated at his cheerfulness.

The next day as they sat on the bench adjacent to the Bay Bridge watching the sparkling blue water reflect the sun's rays, the beauty of the day dispelled some of her bitterness. She wore a pale pink turtleneck sweater and grey pants. "You are so gorgeous!" Stephen had exclaimed upon seeing her. She edged away from the embrace he proferred and sat down putting her purse between them quickly.

He handed her one of the boxed salmon salads they'd purchased at the restaurant. "Stephen, was I some kind of wager?" Stephen started at the bluntness of her comment. "How do you mean?" "What were you betting on when you met me? A slimmer Olivia that you could show off at your firm or was it more than that?" She couldn't bring herself to ask him if he'd conjectured all along to present her as Martha Bates' daughter. She felt a sense of revulsion, her mind brought back echoes of *"I can spell Madeleine for you if you come and sit here."* She closed her salad.

"You've eaten nothing!" Stephen exclaimed as he saw her. "Here you can finish it if you want. I am full." He looked at her. She was looking practically thin now. He hadn't eaten anything since the night before and proceeded to dig into her salad as well. She knew Stephen couldn't be responsible for Uncle Paul but he was responsible for himself, for the shenanigans, for perhaps carrying on elsewhere with other women, two and three timing her. She suddenly felt a huge sense of liberation. In fact she felt vindicated that he was this variously drawn to women, that his attention wandered so automatically from woman to woman, no matter who he was with, it was something he couldn't help but by that same measure, she felt she didn't owe him anything for initiating her weight loss. She felt rightfully light and justified in not wanting to see him anymore.

"I can't see you anymore Stephen." She said bluntly. "Please don't be angry with me Gorgeous!" His look of consternation didn't thaw her resolve, nor did his imploring eyes.

She saw two young women about to pass them and saw Stephen's eyes instinctively follow them, his eyes taking in their figures, measuring their asses. 'Assessing' them. "Stephen, you will find so many more worthwhile projects than me." She said and got up to leave with her purse. He was left with two salad boxes. He quickly pushed them into a bin, wiped his hands and mouth with a napkin and followed her.

It can't be happening he thought. How could his careful plan come apart without any mistakes on his part? Hadn't he done everything right? He knew for a fact that Anil hadn't ratted on him, he just was not capable of doing that. What was this newfound intelligence that Olivia had come upon that had gotten her so riled up and angry with him? His future was coming unglued, that is if any of us were equipped with a way to gluing it in the first place. Well, that's what he'd thought wasn't it? Wasn't he the glue maker?

She in turn was angered by his ability to be distracted by other women even when they were in the middle of breaking up. It was inexorable. A habit that may or may not fade with age she thought. He was so accustomed to having a roving eye that he couldn't stop himself, anymore than he could stop himself batting his eyelids. And, she thought, if he is so swerved by anything in a skirt, it's quite possible he had a woman in every port. The thought hit her like a brick. She wasn't even that unique. There were several more like her. She felt awfully used. No, she didn't owe Stephen anything for her new body. She was just a rung in his social ladder that he would have climbed to reach above and maybe even leave her behind for a better prize someday. Who knew?

She stopped on her tracks. Anil. She would never have run into Anil if it hadn't been for Stephen. She didn't feel she could call him, no matter how angry she was with Stephen. It just wasn't something she could bring herself to do.

Stephen walked slowly back to his office. He saw that he'd missed two calls, one from Anil and the other from Emma Joy. Anil was updating him on a meeting they had at 4pm that day and Emma Joy left him a tearful message, "Stephen, someone rear ended my car. My elbow was resting on the armrest and I seem to have cracked it with the impact and I have terrible whiplash, when are you coming to visit?" Her voice had an unattractive plaintiveness to it. Stephen deleted her message impatiently.

Stephen was convinced whatever it was that had rankled with Olivia could be sorted out. He couldn't believe how much the girl had changed. She had begun to push back, "it's ungainly when women push back so much." He'd said to her once when she had insisted she wanted to spend the evening alone, when he was in San Francisco. "How so?" Her voice had taken on a condescending note. *Hadn't Uncle Paul said to her that her tea party would be ruined if she told anyone of what happened?* Stephen quickly flashed her a smile and apologized, "Of course I didn't mean that Gorgeous!" He'd kissed her on her forehead and had walked some way with her and before they knew it they were at her apartment. They went in and she had snuck into his arms readily, relishing his cooing and his arousing touch, running her hand over his smooth head, caressing his ears, nibbling at them. He felt he had the power to draw her back. He knew she loved when he made love to her. Even though his first few forays with her, he'd made an effort, moving past the folds of her flesh that he wished he could remove with his hand, he'd later started to get deeply aroused by the expression in her eyes, the smile lurking at the surface, the way her eyes half closed at his touch as she leaned into him to join herself in a union that gave her unbridled pleasure.

After the meeting with Anil that evening Stephen asked him what he was doing for dinner. Anil couldn't stop himself "I was hoping if you weren't busy, we could take Olivia out to dinner tonight." Stephen's jaw tightened. He looked absorbed with his email. Emma Joy's tearful voice rang in his ear, he felt he had to get away, however briefly, to recover from the *Olivia Catastrophe* he was experiencing right now. "Er, I might have to leave for Denver tonight, I will see if I can get a flight out."

Anil's eyes widened, "Denver?" "Well, something personal has come up, I will be back on Thursday morning and you can always email me as well."

They went on to review some of their files, responding to belligerent emails from their high paying but very demanding client in New York. They worked through the afternoon in silence. At the end of the afternoon, as Stephen made to leave, Anil looked up at him. "I wonder if *I* can take Olivia out to that dingy little Indian restaurant again then?" he looked at Stephen with his half question, half statement. "You should check with her on that, she can be quite temperamental that girl." Stephen couldn't stop himself.

He had sensed how Olivia responded to Anil the few times they'd met. What had caused her to change her mind about *him* though? Was it something Anil might have said? He counted Anil among his closer colleagues and didn't think he would poach from Stephen's *'chickdex'* no, *'girldex'* but who could tell? Stephen loved coining his various quizzical adjectives, he saw them as assets in relatable phrases, takes smarts to do that he told himself. Any way you cut it, he'd transformed Olivia, such undertakings were risky propositions precisely because of the potential for risks, for things flipping on him, of life thumbing its nose at him. Hadn't it happened with Sandra? Stephen questioned himself.

Olivia was now irresistibly attractive, her body so svelte but her demeanor still under a shier garb, still getting used to her 'lessness.' Stephen's influence had created an edginess that added a verve to her hitherto predictable personality, her innate discretion. Anil, a young, single, overworked lawyer who had been openly impressed with Olivia from the very beginning had started to nestle in Olivia's thoughts despite the barely perceptible but present twitch of his left eye or perhaps because of it. It seemed to only enhance his appeal, making him nerdy, intelligent yet touchable, reachable. She had felt a constant urge to smooth down the long, black hairs on his hands. To put her hands on top of his to see how much bigger his hands were. "Yeah, check with her." Stephen said strapping his heavy bag on and striding out, bemused by his day and confused as to why he was beating a retreat for Denver. Was it really to see Emma Joy in her hour of need? Whose hour of need was it really?

Anil nodded assertively, "I will." He looked through his email contacts to find Olivia's email and started to type, "Tonight." And muttering more to himself than to Stephen, "If she agrees." Stephen stopped short, looked at him briefly, paused as if to say something and proceeded without comment.

Anil could see a possible courtship blossoming between him and Olivia like coming out of a challenging and curved road to be able to finally see straight ahead on one of those interminable highways that connected so many disparate parts of the country.

Stephen walked slowly back into his office and dropped his bag in the chair and slinging his jacket over his shoulder muttered to an empty room that he would be right back and wandered out. He strolled bloodlessly toward the Embarcadero. Unaccustomed to this unhurried pace, he looked down at his shoes and watched how his shoe pointed slightly inward, one step in front of the other, this was news to him, he'd never realized his foot pointed slightly inward when he walked. He was surprised enough to pause inquisitively. Was he observing someone else's feet moving forward?

He didn't notice the typical early afternoon din he was surrounded by, automatically stopping at stoplights and waiting for the walk sign before crossing. He kept walking down the length of the water and walked on a pier jutting into the water. Was water reflective or did we just reflect in it he wondered. He looked down at the dull gray waves lapping against the dark wood of the pier. Life-forms seemed to thrive everywhere in and out of the water. He recalled a conversation with a client of his in Denver, why don't you lead our internal legal team Stephen? He'd asked him and Stephen had shuddered at the thought, he couldn't fathom the boredom of not living in New York City.

How predictable his days would be and…*Where* in Denver? Which neighborhood? What would he do there? The sun was emerging reluctantly and he crossed over to the other side of the pier now able to view his reflection in the slow moving water. He felt the waters were washing his face as he saw his features sway gently, shouldn't baths and showers have that capacity to cleanse? Erase the stains of disappointment? Wasn't there a way to wash this pain in bleach? He marveled at how completely alone he was in this small but packed city. He sat as if at the edge of the world, looking in.

His thoughts seemed to circle around all the possibilities he had considered in his profession. Heavily armed with a star-studded resume, the choices he'd made had been as methodical and thought through as his preparation for the SATs in grade school and for the LSATs later on. He couldn't think of anything he'd done wrong. He'd done everything to avoid making mistakes, meticulous, deliberate and upright, he told himself. That's what he was, an upright man. He stopped and wondered if it mattered that he was upright. How upright had he been? Was there another word he could use instead? Did it matter?

He realized vaguely that it was now quite late in the afternoon and he had walked several miles following a path by the water. He stood transfixed and in thrall of the moment. His moment. All he had striven for, the frenzy of life culminating in the softness of a fading San Francisco light. He wasn't betraying his New

York. He was convinced about that but that San Francisco should offer to serenade him with this swan song? Was he switching loyalties? He shrugged.

The water lapping against the rocks below seemed to lure him with a silver-tongued beckon looking sincere and welcoming. He was utterly free to get cleansed, to get that washing, there was something eager about the face looking up at him from below, a look of familiar welcome. All his life he'd loved this carefully crafted vision. Now he felt obliged to heed this hearken; the perfect svelte legs striding in front of him in pink pumps, the swish of the grey chiffon dress, high above the knees.

What was wrong with being drawn to perfection? Also, he *had* tried everything else hadn't he? His head bobbed in the image of itself as the water moved in general agreement with him. He leaned forward and met the waters that swished and called to him wearing that very same shade of that gray skirt exuding the same allure he had encountered on a New York street not so long ago, imbued with the colors of his painting yielding to the water, spreading, disintegrating.

THIN

ABOUT THE AUTHOR

Sadhana Seelam is a writer and political blogger. She has written three novels, *Surveyor of Properties*, *Thin* and *Two Ruby-like Daughters and One Stray Donkey*. Her screenplays include *Eiffel's Secret*, *Betty & Matieho* and *Getting Published*. Her collection of short stories is entitled *Ginger Garlic* and her poetry collection is called *Pulling a Chariot With My Teeth*. Sadhana divides her time between San Francisco and Hyderabad.